SUGAR PROTECTOR

SUGAR DADDIES #8

CHARITY PARKERSON

Sugar Protector
Sugar Daddies #8
Charity Parkerson

--Warning: This book is intended for readers over the age of 18.

Editor: BZ Hercules & Consultants
ISBN: 978-1-946099-44-0

❀ Created with Vellum

INTRODUCTION

THEY BASED THEIR RELATIONSHIP ON A
CONTRACT. THAT DOESN'T MEAN IT ISN'T LOVE.

Almost three years ago, Jonah threw everything to the wind and joined a sugar daddy website. At the time, he cared less about who took care of him as long as someone cared about him. He never expected his very first contract would the only one he'd ever need.

John Green has money and loves spending it. After all, he works hard. He deserves all the best comforts in life. Becoming someone's sugar daddy, ensuring he gets what he wants when he wants it, doesn't embarrass him in the least. He's paid the bills for more than one younger lover over the years. Jonah is the first to make him want to be wanted for himself, and not his money.

John and Jonah have been a love match from day one. Fate will have to shake things up to get these stubborn men to admit to feeling a single thing.

ONE

Candlelight flickered across the pages of Jonah's open textbook. The words blurred and ran together in the shitty lighting. If he possessed a single ounce of sense, he would've told John no when the man invited him over tonight. He should've known no studying would occur. Almost three years ago, Jonah had met John on a website that connected sugar daddies with younger men. From their first date, they'd hit things off. Jonah was in a weird spot with the man now, a place where he didn't want things to ever end, but he could never confess as much.

On his stomach and with his chin resting on his crossed arms, Jonah tried concentrating harder on his studies. A breeze skirted over the small of Jonah's back as John pushed his shirt higher. Warm lips brushed the spot he bared.

"I thought you were helping me study. You know these tests determine whether I graduate. I'm already graduating a year later than I expected." If he graduated at all, Jonah silently added.

A soft chuckle vibrated against his skin. Jonah's eyes fell closed and his dick hardened at the sensation. A pant escaped him. Everything about John was amazing. He had such a giving and beautiful heart Jonah would've fallen for the man, even if he wasn't the sexiest man on the planet, but John was that too. He was dark-haired with a touch of gray and large—like a muscular mountain. John was six feet and four inches of solid steel. Jonah was tall too, but not that tall, and he was skinny. John made him feel protected in every way—like the world could never touch him. Even when the man acted like a two-year-old on crack, which happened quite often, Jonah loved him. It was his deepest secret.

"I'm helping," John said, easing Jonah's swim trunks lower, and baring part of Jonah's ass. "What's twenty-three plus forty-six?"

Jonah rolled his eyes at the childish question. "Sixty-nine."

John's teeth sank into his now bare ass cheek. "Exactly. Such an awesome number. See? I'm helping."

"Except I'm studying Chemistry," Jonah said, dropping his forehead on his crossed arms and sucking in a breath.

"That's a good topic too. We have that. You'll do great."

Jonah wanted to argue, but he also wanted everything John did to him. On a massive steel-framed lounge built for three and covered in a thick mattress, Jonah had his books spread around him, doing his damnedest to hang on to his sanity. The waterfall running into the gorgeous swimming pool drowned out the world. The thick foliage and high fences kept them hidden from view. John had gone out his way to make the setting romantic. He always treated Jonah like it was okay for Jonah to let everything go because John would always take care of him. The problem was, they were a contract, not a couple. Jonah needed a real education to get a real job, so when John got bored with him, he'd be okay. A shot of pain hit Jonah in the chest at the thought.

His shorts tugged lower, stealing away everything but the sensation of John's lips on his skin.

"Keep studying," John said, even as he stripped Jonah bare. "I want your eyes on the page."

Each breath Jonah took came harder than the last as he tried to do as John demanded. His gaze moved back to the chemistry book, but he saw nothing.

"On your knees."

Jonah got his knees beneath him while he stared at his book. His entire focus locked on John's every move. John's lips and teeth explored each of Jonah's cheeks. His thumb skimmed Jonah's asshole. Jonah dropped his forehead to his forearm again. A stinging slap landed on his ass. "You're studying. Get back to it."

Jonah went back to staring at the open book while seeing nothing. John's lips caressed the spot he'd smacked, kissing away the sting. He fingered Jonah's asshole. Jonah's dick leaked onto the lounge. Then John's tongue replaced his fingers. Jonah fought the urge to drop his head again. The light brush of the man's tongue circling his asshole was making Jonah insane. More pre-cum dripped from his cock. He was so turned on, he couldn't think. John didn't let up. He licked and probed until Jonah writhed, wanting more. John massaged Jonah's balls and dick, bringing him closer to the edge. Jonah didn't dare move his eyes from the book. He didn't want John to stop.

John shifted onto his knees. Jonah held his breath. He barely heard the crinkle of the condom wrapper. Cool liquid swiped across his asshole before something hard pressed against it. He was beyond fucking ready for John to fuck him hard. Everything about John was massive. They never had sex without tons of foreplay. The first time he'd seen John's dick had been a big nope moment for Jonah. He'd been certain he couldn't take it. Now John always made him want to beg for it.

John pushed his way inside, stretching Jonah wide. A gasp tore for Jonah's lips as a moan fell from John's. Jonah's dick pumped out pre-cum like it was painting the cushion beneath them. John adjusted angles and rocked forward. Damn, he always fucked Jonah perfectly, hitting the right spot.

"You're so goddamn sexy. All I want to do is be inside this ass all the time. Everything about you is perfect."

Jonah couldn't take it. He reached between his legs and tugged his cock. "Damn, John. Like that. Don't stop," Jonah begged as John continued massaging Jonah's insides at the perfect angle with his dick. He squeezed his eyes shut and focused on the building pressure. His hips moved in time with John's thrusts. They were perfect together. Three years had done nothing but give them all the practice they needed to learn how to please each other without thought. It was like they'd been made for each other.

John's fingers dug into his skin, proving how close he was getting. "Fuck. Jesus. Come for me, Jonah. You feel too good. I can't hold back."

Jonah pumped at his cock, pulling and stroking, driving closer to oblivion. The pressure climbed and built, combining with the way John filled him and pleased him. His lungs seized. Everything went quiet. Lights popped behind his closed lids like fireworks as the pressure turned into ecstasy. His entire body jerked as his orgasm hit. He kept tugging at his dick, needing every spasm.

"Holy shit," John cried, stiffening and letting Jonah's orgasm milk his cock into giving up his explosion—like he always did. Jonah knew him. Knew his body. He cried out in pleasure, filling Jonah with pride. John collapsed, rolling to the side at the last second, sparing Jonah most of his weight. He squeezed Jonah against his chest. His ragged breaths caressed the shell of Jonah's ear. "You're like the other half of me."

Jonah's eyes fell closed at John's words. His throat swelled. It was as close to I love you that he'd ever get, and the words always stabbed Jonah through the heart. He was so fucking in love with John, it choked him. Jonah had to swallow it down. They'd never be that couple. Jonah was arm candy until John traded him in for a newer model—like a car. Except the car had feelings and Jonah's heart broke every time he thought about it. The worst part of the whole thing was—if John lost everything tomorrow, Jonah would still want him, and it mattered not at all to anyone but him.

Minutes passed. Jonah made no attempt to move away. John's steady heartbeat caressed Jonah's ear. He pressed closer to the sound, soaking up John's warmth.

John stroked his hair and kissed his temple. "By the way, David Baker is having a grand opening event tomorrow at noon. You know the deal—bad conversation and even worse champagne. I'll pick you up at eleven thirty."

An exasperated chuckle rose in Jonah's throat. Even to his ears, it sounded tired as it fell from his lips. "Baby, why have I been trying to study all night?

I have a test tomorrow." Jonah shifted to his knees and straddled John's hips. He kissed John's chest. His eyes flipped up, meeting John's sexy green gaze. "As much as I would love to go, I can't miss my exam."

"It's fine," John said, sounding petulant and making Jonah smile. "I'll jump on the sugar daddy website later and hire someone to go with me. It's not a big deal."

Ouch. Jonah kept his lips pressed to John's chest, hoping to hide his wince. It wasn't like he could complain. This wasn't a real relationship. The pains in his chest didn't matter. John wasn't his. The man was free to do whatever and whoever he wanted. That didn't stop it from cutting Jonah to the bone. "I can see you afterward, if you're not too worn out from an even younger man." Jonah tried infusing as much humor as he could into the claim. He'd be damned if John saw how much it hurt.

John's fingers swiped through his hair. "You're my favorite everything. You know that. Just text me when you're free and I'll pick you up." John's massive arms encircled Jonah and squeezed. "Ugh. I miss you already. You're supposed to be all about me."

Jonah's throat swelled. He wished John's words

meant more and came from the heart. All he could do was continue kissing John's chest. This was all he had of his giant lover. It had to be enough. Fuck studying. He wanted every second of John he could get.

TWO

THE NEIGHBORHOOD WHERE JOHN'S BROTHER Jude lived with his husband Hendrix was quaint. It fit his brother's personality. Jude had always preferred peace over extravagance. Luckily, he'd still chosen a much younger and hot husband. Otherwise, John would've been forced to disown him. Not really. He loved Jude. John also realized he was lucky to be so close with his only sibling. A lot of people didn't speak to their siblings at all. John saw his almost daily. Jude owned the company that had made them rich. There'd been no real reason for Jude to bring him onboard, sharing the wealth, other than he wanted to do so. He knew Jude told everyone John had made Green's Fighter Fuel a success with his massive wheeling and dealing skills, but still, Jude could've stopped at giving him a modest salary and kept the rest for himself. Instead, he'd been beyond generous in his salary plus shares, making John a partial owner. Together, they'd worked hard, and it paid off. They were set for life, even if they quit now.

Still, no one would look at this neighborhood and peg Jude as a millionaire. The houses were all single-family homes. They were cute but small. As John jogged up Jude's front steps, he could picture Jude being happy here. His gaze swung toward the porch swing. It was just big enough for two. An image of Jonah and him filled John's mind. He could see Jonah tucked against his side, his dark hair reflecting the sunlight while his sexy light-brown gaze held John's. They could be happy here too—right on top of each other. John knew that was exactly why this place appealed to Jude. He lived here with the love of his life.

Hendrix opened the door before John fell down a rabbit hole in his mind. "Hey."

John blinked, pulling back from the edge of admitting something to himself he didn't like to think about. "Hey."

The tiny strawberry blond who'd stolen his brother's heart smiled. "Jude called and said you were on your way over. I have to admit, I'm surprised by the invitation to join you today. Don't you have ten teenagers on speed dial for this?" Hendrix's light emerald eyes shone bright with mirth as he made the claim.

Only because John knew Hendrix was joking did he laugh. He knew Hendrix thought Jonah was way too young for him. After all, from day one, the guy hadn't hidden his thoughts. "Only one and he has school today."

"How is Jonah doing?" Hendrix asked, pulling the door closed behind him.

"He's good. How are you doing?" About a year and a half earlier, Hendrix had lost a leg. No one could tell it today. He walked without as much as limp in his prosthetic.

"I'm good. Ready for Jude to get back from Texas, but good."

That was the reason John had chosen Hendrix to go with him today. With Jonah busy and Jude out of town, they needed something to keep them out of trouble. John more than Hendrix, but whatever. "I'm surprised you didn't go with Jude to Texas," John said, leading Hendrix to the passenger side of his Hummer. He opened the door for Hendrix.

"I had a doctor's appointment. I tried

rescheduling, but they couldn't fit me in for three more months. Since I can't go that long between appointments yet, I had to miss going with Jude."

Hendrix's response had a hundred other questions running through John's mind. He asked each one on the drive to David Baker's latest location. Jonah was used to John's nonstop talking. Hendrix wasn't. By the time they arrived at the organic food restaurant, Hendrix looked ready to stitch John's lips closed. John knew the look. It was the same one he got from everyone except Jonah.

He tried to hold his tongue to give Hendrix a break. John lasted until they cleared the front door. "There's our client," John said, spotting the blond man with graying temples across the room.

David spotted him at the same time and met him halfway. Even the man's light blue eyes smiled. "John, how are you? I'm glad you could make it."

John returned the man's smile as they shook hands. He genuinely liked David. "I'm good. You know I never miss one of your grand openings if I can help it."

David's gaze slid Hendrix's way before moving back to John. "Where's Jonah?"

A chuckle rose in John's throat. Jonah would get a kick out of this story. "He has an exam today he couldn't miss, but he sends his best. You know he hates missing your parties. Luckily, my brother-in-law was free today. David, this is Jude's husband, Hendrix. Hendrix meet David Baker. David was one of our very first clients."

They shook hands. David looked genuinely relieved Jonah hadn't been tossed over. John made a mental note tell Jonah all about this later. No doubt Jonah would listen to the recount with all the patience Hendrix lacked.

"Jude never comes to anything. It's a good thing John brought you along or we never would've met." David laughed at his own joke.

"You know Jude. He loves working on sponsorships and whatnot, but doesn't do the parties," John pointed out, saving Hendrix. He understood Hendrix didn't usually go to these events.

David nodded. "You know, I don't think I realized Jonah was still in college," he said, immediately dismissing Hendrix as someone he'd never see again. "Where does he go?"

"Stanford."

David's smile turned even brighter. "My alma mater. What's his major?"

John's mind blanked. Did he know? Had he ever asked? Had Jonah ever said?

"He's studying to be a chemist," Hendrix said, jumping in.

John's gaze swung Hendrix's way. "He is?" Even John heard the disbelief in his tone. He scrambled to hide his ignorance. Luckily, someone else had already snagged David's attention.

"Excuse me," David said, getting pulled in the opposite direction. "Please enjoy the party. It was good meeting you, Hendrix."

John and Hendrix nodded at David. The moment he was out of earshot, John was right back in it. "Is Jonah studying to be a chemist?"

Hendrix shrugged. "How the fuck should I know? I was just trying to save you from looking like a dumbass. It's obvious that guy likes Jonah, and you were a half second away from having to admit you don't even know what he's studying. How do you not know what Jonah's major is, by the way? How long have you been seeing each other?"

John tried calculating in his head before giving up. "I don't know. A few years."

Hendrix shook his head, looking horrified. "Do the two of you ever talk or do you just fuck all the time?"

Although John realized Hendrix wasn't in love with the whole sugar daddy deal, he hadn't realized Hendrix felt quite this much distaste over the matter. "We talk." At least, John talked. Mostly, Jonah listened and interjected just enough to keep John talking. "We're friends." Weren't they? Fuck. Now Hendrix had him questioning everything. He'd do better. Just because John hadn't realized he was neglecting some aspects of Jonah's care didn't mean he couldn't fix it. "Do you have any plans for the yacht in the next few days?"

Hendrix blinked at the sudden change in topic. "No."

John gave him a sharp nod. "Good. I think I'll take it out." John and Jude split the cost of a yacht and took turns using it. In truth, John used it more than Jude.

Hendrix shook his head and kept his thoughts to himself. That was fine. Once John got an idea, he had to set things in motion or it drove him nuts. He pulled out his phone and shot off a quick text to Jonah.

John: *I hope your test went well. When you get home, pack a bag. Make sure you have Cricket ready to go with us too.*

Jonah: *Why am I packing a bag?*

John: *We're taking the yacht out.*

No response came for several minutes, setting John's teeth on edge. By the time his phone buzzed, he was ready to growl and stamp his feet to have his way.

Jonah: *I'll be waiting with bells on.*

A smile tugged at John's lips. They were good. Perfect, in fact. He shouldn't let a small thing like not knowing Jonah's major get under his skin. After all, John could spend the next few days asking questions. He could make up for lost time. It wasn't like he didn't know Jonah. He knew exactly how to make Jonah moan. That counted for a lot. Didn't it?

———

PROFESSOR MUNICH WALKED with an odd gait that couldn't be mistaken for anyone else. Strangely, he moved fast for such an old man. By the time Jonah caught up with him, he was practically running to match the man's pace.

"Professor Munich, hold up." At his call, Jonah swore he saw the man's already sagging shoulders droop.

He pushed his glasses up his nose as he turned, waiting for Jonah to reach his side. His gray mustache twitched. Jonah had a bad feeling it was in disgust. "Mr. Young, what can I do for you?"

Jonah didn't beat around the bush. "Is there any way I can find out my test score early?"

The elderly man sucked in a breath, making a show of how Jonah obviously made him tired. "Is there some reason you can't wait like the rest of the class?"

"I have to go out of town."

Dead air stretched between them. Munich rocked back on his heels and clasped his hands in front of him. "Mr. Young, have you ever considered that college might not be for you?" He had, but that still seemed a rude thing to say. Jonah opened his mouth to defend himself. The professor kept talking, cutting him from the conversation. "There are a lot of students who not only manage to make it here every day, they also recognize how lucky they are to be here in the first place. Do you have any idea how many people are denied entry into this university every year?" Jonah didn't, but he assumed it was a lot, and he recognized the question as rhetorical. "Yet, somehow you slipped through the cracks. To answer your question, I do not yet know your score, but does it matter? Really?"

Jonah dipped his chin, ignoring the tightness in

his chest. "Thank you for your time." It seemed it didn't matter if he spent the rest of the week on a trip with John. There wasn't a single soul that believed Jonah had a chance in hell at graduating, including himself.

AN ODD JOLT of nervousness overcame John as he used his elbow to ring Jonah's doorbell. He fought the urge to feel of his hair and make sure it wasn't standing on end. Thankfully, he didn't have a hand to spare. The door swung open. Jonah held Cricket, ensuring the tiny dog couldn't dart out. His eyes lit as they landed on John. John's already racing heart skipped a beat. It seemed he should be past this part after almost three years together. He was considerably older than Jonah. Old enough to be his dad, in fact. Jonah wouldn't want him forever. One day, sooner rather than later, John would truly look his age while Jonah was still young and sexy. Someone closer to his age would turn Jonah's head and their deal would be at an end. John promised himself he wouldn't regret Jonah when that day came.

"Hey, gorgeous."

That day wasn't today, John reminded himself as Jonah's sultry voice washed over him. John's usual smile pulled at his lips at the simple knowledge he'd soon be holding Jonah. "Hey, baby."

Jonah pushed the screen door open for him. "What's all that?" Jonah asked, nodding toward the items in John's hands while struggling to hang on to a wiggling Cricket.

John waited until Jonah closed the door and set Cricket free before holding out the flowers for him. "An assortment of wild flowers to match your spirit, and," he held out the box, "chocolate cake for my sexy sweetheart."

"Awww," Jonah cooed, accepting both. He sniffed the flowers before peering inside the box. "Yum. That smells delicious. You'll make me fat before long."

John's brows snapped together without his permission. "You know I'm not with you because of how you look, right? I don't care how much you weigh." It was true. Jonah was so goddamn beautiful on the inside, he could look like anything on the outside and it wouldn't matter. He'd still be breathtaking.

Jonah winked. "You say that now, because I haven't eaten this cake yet." Jonah headed for the kitchen. John tried following, but Cricket scratched the legs of his jeans, slowing him down.

John scooped up the dog and chased after Jonah. "I'm rarely allowed anything good, since I sell health food for a living, but I like making you happy. Eat the cake and don't think about the calories. Okay?"

After setting the box on the counter, Jonah glanced over, smiling. "I was joking, baby. What's bothering you today? Did the guy you hired to go with you to the Baker's party leave you unsatisfied?"

The gibe didn't help John's exasperation. Jonah didn't sound the least bit jealous. John would snap a dude's neck if he found out anyone else touched Jonah. Yet Jonah joked about John being with someone else as if it didn't matter. Yeah, for a while, they'd enjoyed some wild times, inviting a third into their relationship and whatnot, but those days were over. At least, he thought they were. "You know I was joking when I said that last night, right? I only wanted you to feel guilty so you'd come with me. I took Hendrix."

Something flashed in Jonah's eyes, but he turned away too quickly for John to puzzle it out. Jonah snagged a vase from the cabinet and filled it with water. He kept his gaze locked on his task. "How is Hendrix?"

The hint of sadness in Jonah's voice bothered John. Something was off about them today. They felt out of rhythm. "He's fine. How are you?"

"Fine," Jonah said, flashing him a smile that looked forced to John.

John stroked Cricket's fur one more time and kissed his head before setting him at his feet. This time when the dog fought to climb him, John stepped over him and closed the distance between Jonah and him. As his chest collided with Jonah's back, he reached past him and turned off the water. Jonah didn't move. John could practically feel him holding his breath. The skin peeking out above Jonah's collar at his shoulder called to John. He dropped his mouth, kissing the bared skin. The sound of Jonah's breath catching sounded loud in the otherwise silent kitchen. He tugged Jonah's shirt sleeve, baring more of Jonah's shoulder. He kissed that spot. Jonah melted into him. John's dick stirred. He hadn't meant for the moment to turn sexual. It was Jonah. The man fit so perfectly in John's arms—like he'd been born to be exactly where John held him. Even their names fit. John and Jonah destined to meet.

John's palms slid around Jonah's sides, caressing until they met at Jonah's stomach. His lips moved higher, lightly brushing until he reached Jonah's ear.

He pressed a light kiss to its shell. "Do you know what I pictured when I saw that cake at the store?"

Jonah sounded a step beyond breathless when he answered. "What?"

John popped the button on Jonah's shorts. He tugged, pulling open the zipper one tooth at a time, dragging out Jonah's anticipation. "I saw myself smearing it all over your body before I went down on you and do you know what?"

A whimper escaped Jonah. "What?"

"You made it taste twice as sweet," John said, pushing Jonah's shorts down before exploding into action. He snagged Jonah around the hips and spun him before easily lifting him onto the counter. "I'm too old to get on my knees." That was all the explanation John offered before he bent and sucked Jonah. Jonah cried out as his cock slipped down John's throat. Jonah whipped off his shirt before scratching at John's shoulders. He leaned back as far as the cabinets hanging behind him would let him and pumped against John's lips. John chuckled around Jonah's dick. He knew he had the man trapped in an awkward position, making it impossible for Jonah to control the rhythm. John liked having Jonah at his mercy. Maybe bad knees came with age, but so did patience and skill. He licked and sucked, hollowing out his cheeks and going for quick results. When he felt Jonah's muscles tense, he pulled away and captured the man's lips. An evil chuckle rose in his throat when Jonah tried biting him in his frustration. His cock twitched in his jeans. He wanted to bury himself in Jonah and never come up for air. Right now, he needed to let Jonah know, in the only way he could, this was more than a deal between them. John could never say the words. When Jonah left him for someone his own age, John didn't want him to feel guilty. But he needed Jonah to remember that John had made him happy while they were together. Jonah needed to remember John had worked hard for them every day.

After a quick nip at Jonah's bottom lip, John flipped open the cake box and swiped at the icing. He held his finger out to Jonah. Jonah didn't disappoint. While holding John's stare with his hungry gaze, he closed his lips around John's finger and sucked. John's dick leaked in his jeans like it was the thing in Jonah's mouth. John lured Jonah's forward as Jonah continued licking away the icing. The moment he was within striking distance, John recaptured the man's mouth, savoring the flavor of chocolate lingering on Jonah's tongue.

"Mhmm," John hummed. "Damn. It's even

better than I imagined." He swiped at the icing again. This time, he dragged the mess down Jonah's cock before going down on him again.

As male salt and chocolate coated his taste buds, Jonah tugged at his hair, taking his pleasure. Moans filled the air, making John twice as horny.

"Jesus, John. Yes." Damn, he loved the way his name sounded in that tone. "Just like that. Oh my god."

John thought he'd blow in his jeans just from the sounds Jonah made. He was so sexy. It never got old pleasuring him. He doubled his efforts, massaging Jonah's balls and asshole as he bobbed on his dick.

Jonah's fingers dug into his shoulders. "Don't stop." A whimper rang from the walls. A cry followed. Cum flooded his mouth and rolled down his chin. John swallowed as fast as he could while Jonah rocked against his tongue, riding out every wave. John kissed a path up Jonah's stomach, swiping his face on the man's skin. When he reached Jonah's mouth, Jonah accepted his kiss and the taste of his own cum without hesitation. John's lust skyrocketed. He had no intention of acting on it, though. This was all about Jonah. John had some making up to do. Hendrix made him realize he'd been selfish. That ended today. John made a silent vow. By the time they were finished with this trip, he would know all there was to know about Jonah, and Jonah would be first from now on.

ON HIS STOMACH, nude, and sprawled across John's lap in bed, Jonah wondered if his dick would ever work again. He was completely drained, and John was still teasing him. They'd turned a movie on half an hour ago. The rocking of the boat tried putting him to sleep. John's touch kept him awake. His fingers dug into Jonah's lower back, massaging before moving lower. He skimmed Jonah's crack before rubbing his cheeks and moving back to his lower back. The man's huge erection kept tapping his side. Jonah had no clue how John was still hard. He knew he should try harder to make John as tired as he was, but Jonah couldn't move. Exhaustion and John's hands on his skin kept him paralyzed.

"You're beautiful," John whispered as he skimmed Jonah's crack again. This time, he delved deeper, pressing on Jonah's asshole with the perfect amount of pressure. "I could touch you all night." He fingered Jonah's ass as he made the claim.

A pant escaped Jonah. Despite being half dead,

his dick stirred. "You're killing me. Tell me what you need and it's yours."

"Tell me how your test went."

"About as well as can be expected," Jonah answered, blowing off the question.

John's fingers disappeared and reappeared wet, easily slipping inside him. A moan choked Jonah. He massaged at the perfect angle. Jonah fought the urge to hump John's lap. "What's that supposed to mean? Tell me again what you're studying."

It was like some new age torture method. John toyed with his body while talking about things Jonah didn't care to discuss. "It means I probably failed. Engineering is my major."

John froze. Jonah whimpered. At the sound, John went back to playing. "Why engineering?"

Jonah turned his head and twisted at an angle so he could see John's face. "Why the sudden interest?"

John shrugged. "I'm curious. You don't strike me as the engineering type. I mean, that doesn't sound interesting and you're interesting."

A chuckle shook Jonah's body. It turned into a moan as John's fingers pushed deeper. "Jesus. Like that." Jonah couldn't have stopped the plea if he tried. John knew how to make him beg. "If I make you fly, will you promise to come to Mom's with me on Sunday for Mother's Day?"

Jonah considered biting him. "You don't have to fucking tease me for that. Of course I'll go."

John froze again. "Wait. What about your mom? I've never met her. Are you ashamed of me?"

Some things were more important than getting off. The hurt in John's voice had Jonah crawling away from his touch and shifting onto his knees facing John. "No, baby. I could never be ashamed of you." He straddled John's lap and kissed his neck. "Don't say anything like that again." He moved down John's body. It was time for him to take care of that huge erection that had been trying to get his attention. He had to distract John from this line of questioning. They couldn't talk about his mom. Jonah never wanted John to know that ugliness. They were beautiful. He had to keep this one place where he was good enough.

JONAH HADN'T ANSWERED HIM. It was the first time John had ever noticed it was intentional. Even though Jonah claimed he wasn't ashamed, his actions said otherwise. There had to be a reason

Jonah wasn't really answering his questions. People only did that when they were hiding something. He didn't want to be the something Jonah hid.

Jonah moved lower down the bed, kissing John's stomach and heading for his erection. John couldn't let that happen. He wasn't stupid enough to think he could stand against Jonah once the guy had John's dick in his mouth. Jonah was too perfect. He knew exactly how to keep John.

"I'm trying to talk to you," John said with a laugh, tugging Jonah back into his lap.

Jonah huffed as he settled in and wrapped his arms around John's neck. He looked adorably frustrated as he held John's stare. "Why do you want to know all this?" Even though Jonah still had the same playful tone, there was something else John couldn't pinpoint tinging his voice.

"Because I care," John said, refusing to back down. "You don't talk to me about school or your family. It's like you don't really want me to be part of your life."

Jonah's smile fell. "Of course I want you in my life. Trust me, you really don't want to know this." There it was. That hidden tone was full-on now. Jonah wasn't joking. He didn't want to tell John anything.

John had to know. "Yes I do."

"Okay," Jonah said, scooting closer so their erections bumped. "If you have to know, there's no sense in doing anything for my mom for Mother's Day. She won't accept anything from me. She also hasn't spoken a word to me in five years. I still go see her every few months, so she can ignore me in person, but—after this last time—I think I'm done trying." John's stomach dropped at the matter-of-fact way Jonah talked about something that obviously hurt him. Jonah kept going. "It also doesn't matter how I did on my test. There's no chance in hell I'll graduate this year. I think I'm done trying to force that too."

"Why?"

Jonah shrugged. "Why what? Why does my mom hate me or why am I failing? The answer for both is probably the same. Maybe I'm just a failure."

"Okay. Now that's bullshit," John said, feeling his temper slip.

Jonah ignored him. "My mom had a beautiful life planned out for me where I married the girl I dated through high school and had lots of kids. Then, she found out that girl had boy parts, and—suddenly —I was no longer her child. As to school, I tried my best, but I've missed too many days to keep up. All the passed tests in the world can't save me now."

John shook his head. "What do you mean you've missed too many days? You're always there." At least, it felt like Jonah was always at school. He couldn't touch the story about Jonah's mom yet. He was too enraged.

A bright smile lit Jonah's face. It was completely at odds with his earlier tone. "Where do you think I'm supposed to be today, John? Or tomorrow? Or the week we were in Cancun, or when we went to France or Greece?" Jonah shrugged. "I tried, but it didn't work out for me. It's okay. I never really wanted to be an engineer. My guidance counselor chose what he thought would be my best path with the scholarships I received. I'm not good at it." Jonah shrugged. "In truth, I'm not good at anything. I'm a terrible student and an even worse son. Maybe I'll just go out and get a job so I can be bad at that too."

It was worse than Hendrix made things out to be. John was beyond selfish. He hadn't once considered Jonah's needs. In fact, he'd never even asked if Jonah needed to be elsewhere. He'd simply given Jonah instructions on when to be ready to go—like a paid employee.

John couldn't find his voice. Self-hatred sat on his windpipe.

Jonah shook his head when John didn't speak. A sad smile touched his lips. "I told you that you didn't want to hear it." He leaned in and kissed John's neck. John held him there, seeing nothing. He'd failed Jonah. The massive revelation overwhelmed John. He loved Jonah. In fact, he had for a long time, but now he realized—if he loved him—John needed to act like it and get out of Jonah's way. As long as they were together, John would always want to come first. He was spoiled like that. Jonah would never make a place for himself in the world with an old man like John hanging around his neck, weighing him down. So this was it. It hurt worse than he'd ever expected. He'd enjoy this final trip with Jonah, and then he'd set the man free. Jonah would be great at whatever he did in life, but he'd never find out what that was with John around, stealing everything from him. As he accepted Jonah's kiss, John's heart shattered in his chest. No matter what, Jonah would always be the greatest love of his life. But from here on, he'd love him from a distance.

Jonah pulled away when John didn't react to his kiss. "Do you think so badly of me that you'll ignore me now?" Jonah asked, looking hurt.

John's fingers found Jonah's hair. He stroked. "I could never think badly of you, baby." With a roll and a tuck, he had Jonah pinned beneath him. He poured every ounce of his hurt and longing into their kiss. If this was their last trip, he wanted Jonah to have nothing but good memories. He wanted Jonah to remember how John loved him like no one else ever would. He loved Jonah so much, he'd move out of his way.

THREE

As a knock landed on Jonah's door, he practically skipped to answer. He'd been texting John all morning, trying to figure out what he needed to wear for the Mother's Day thing, but John hadn't gotten back with him. It was hell. He hoped whatever John had planned wasn't fancy. If so, he might not have time to get ready. Confusion rendered Jonah mute as the door swung open. The dark-haired, light-eyed man on the other side was someone he hadn't seen in ages. Jonah scooped up Cricket and pushed the screen door open.

"Brad?" The presence of John's lawyer was more than a surprise. It was downright odd. He'd only seen the man in passing since he'd drawn up the contract between John and him. "What brings you by?"

The way Brad shifted from foot to foot while avoiding eye contact had Jonah's stomach muscles drawing up tight with dread. "I came by to go over Mr. Green's severance package with you."

"His... What?" The ache in the center of Jonah's chest screamed he'd heard the man right, but he couldn't have. Right?

Brad took an audible breath and met Jonah's stare. "Your severance package. Don't worry. John has ensured you're taken care of for a long time."

Several things occurred to Jonah at once. He should invite Brad inside. He'd just been dumped. John had fucking dumped him via his lawyer, and last but not least, Jonah was furious. "I don't want it." He started to close the door in Brad's face.

Brad stuck his foot out, stopping him. "You should hear me out. If you still want to send me away afterward, I can't stop you."

"You can't stop me now," Jonah said, pointing out the obvious while daring Brad with his stare to try.

"Please?"

Jesus. Jonah barely suppressed an eye roll at Brad's begging. John had probably threatened his life if he let Jonah turn him away. "Go on, then. Speak your piece."

Brad looked around. "Here?"

Jonah gave him a short nod. "Here." He wasn't risking not being able to throw the man out later. He damn sure couldn't give John the satisfaction of this lawyer seeing him cry.

After clearing his throat, Brad looked resigned. "Okay. Well, as you may or may not know, the house and car were paid off last year and have always been in your name. They were gifts and Mr. Green would like them to stay that way." As much as Jonah wanted to tell him to shove both up his ass, he didn't relish being homeless, and he wasn't stupid. Maybe. Well, obviously, he was a little dumb. After all, he'd fallen in love with John.

"Okay."

Brad nodded, as if relieved Jonah wouldn't argue. "As to your severance, John would also like you to send him an estimate on how much your college education will be in total through graduation so he can pay off the remainder. He also requests you pick a major you'll actually enjoy. In addition, he's written you a check for two hundred and fifty thousand dollars."

Jonah couldn't breathe. He fought the urge to put his head between his knees and suck air. Falling apart was moments away and Jonah didn't want a witness. He'd never been more grateful he'd never confessed his love. John would never know how he broke Jonah in that moment. He swallowed. Whatever he said now would go straight back to John. Jonah would be goddamned if he looked like a fool in the end.

"Please let John know that I appreciate him not leaving me homeless or without a way to get around. As to the tuition and check, tell him I politely decline. I'm sorry you were placed in such an uncomfortable position."

A sad smile passed over Brad's lips, disappearing as quickly as it appeared. "I'm the one who's sorry, Jonah. For the record, I think he's making a huge mistake. Anyone with eyes can see you care about him. Everyone else uses him, but contracted agreement or not, I honestly don't believe it was ever about the money for you."

It hurt. Jonah's throat swelled. Losing John hurt way more than he ever imagined. "It never mattered how I feel," Jonah admitted, hearing his pain despite his best efforts. He cleared his throat. "Have a nice life, Brad. I've always liked you."

Brad's blush might've made Jonah smile under any other circumstance. Right now, in the face of losing the only thing that mattered, Jonah felt nothing but the shattering of his heart.

"You too, Jonah."

Jonah closed the door and set Cricket on the floor. He pressed his forehead to the cool wood. With his eyes squeezed shut, Jonah tried to squash the image of John's smiling face. It wasn't like he'd ever believed John would marry him or anything like that. In the back of his mind, he'd always known John would get bored and move on. That was what rich, older men did. They didn't settle down. They didn't settle for or on anything. When the money was endless, so too were the newer model toys. It was just that... Well, it was just that Jonah was stupid, apparently. He'd let his heart get touched. A tear rolled down his cheek. Jonah wiped it away.

Cricket scratched at his feet. Jonah stared down at the only thing he had left. John had bought him too. Fuck. Who did things like that for someone they didn't love at all? Things hadn't been perfect. At first, John had been wild. Jonah had done things he didn't like to make him happy—like sharing partners. Jonah scooped Cricket from the floor again and cuddled him. The day John had shown up with the tiny dog, he'd looked at Jonah differently. Jonah thought... It didn't matter what he'd thought. They were done. He was alone. On Mother's Day. If John had hoped to make a point by choosing today, he'd succeeded beautifully. Jonah was acutely aware he'd never mattered at all to anyone, especially to the people he loved the most.

JOHN STARED at an oil painting in a badly lit room, seeing nothing. Not that there was anything to see. He was a great lover of the arts. The museum was one of his favorite places, but this was a cheap painting inside an expensive spa. There was nothing to see here. He was acutely aware of his mother speaking. The thing was, he couldn't force his brain to cling to a single word. His tongue didn't want to work either. Everything felt heavy and wrong. A woman rubbed his feet. Why was she touching him again? He hated everyone's touch, except Jonah's. How strange was that realization? John used to touch everyone he could. Now all he wanted was to be left alone with Jonah.

"What's wrong with you, boy?"

John glanced over at his mom's question. "What?"

She rolled her eyes. "I thought we were having a

mother-son day. All you've done is stare into space."

"I'm fine. This is fun."

Viv snorted. "Bullshit."

"I'll pick a different gift for you next year."

"For fuck's sake. There's nothing wrong with the gift. You know I love the spa." She nodded at the girl massaging her feet. "You know this. Right, girlie?"

"Yes, ma'am," the girl dutifully replied, making John's eyes roll against his will.

"The place is not the problem. The company is. What the hell is wrong with you today? You're never silent. Hell, you're never even semi-silent."

"I'm sorry. What would you like to talk about?"

"Jesus," Viv muttered, sounding irritated. "Where's Jonah? Now that's a boy who knows how to entertain an old lady."

A smile touched John's lips even as a pain sliced through his chest. Jonah knew how to entertain an old man too, but John kept that to himself. Had Brad dropped the news yet? How had Jonah taken it? John couldn't breathe. He blinked at the cheap painting again, seeing nothing.

"Are you even listening to me?"

"Of course, Mother," John said, even though he

hadn't heard a word. "I'm a disappointment. You'll never have grandchildren. Unless, of course, we consider Jonah's age. He's young enough to be your grandson. Did I cover everything?" He didn't need to listen. They rarely spoke of anything else.

"Why didn't you bring Jonah along?" she asked rather than answering. "A lot of people have mothers and a mother-in-law who still manage to visit both on the same day. Did he not want to see me?"

"Stop," John said, hearing the exasperated laugh in his voice and incapable of stopping it. "You know damn well Jonah loves you. Things just didn't work out, okay?"

"Well, that's all you had to say." Viv smiled and started happily chatting with the woman rubbing her feet.

John shook his head and looked away. She didn't understand. His mom loved her dramatics. He didn't know how to explain things hadn't worked out at all. Not just for today. Soon enough, he'd have to tell her. He'd have to tell everyone. John didn't have the words for this. He didn't know how to admit he'd stolen everything from Jonah. While Jonah had been smiling and going out of his way for John in every way, John had been taking and taking, never once noticing that Jonah was drowning. What kind of person was he really? He'd always thought he was a fairly decent human. Yet he'd constantly let Jonah down and never once noticed. Now it was over. John didn't know how to make the pain stop. Maybe it would never go away. It was possible he'd choke on the horrible sensations inside him, die in his sleep, and no one would ever know it was his fault.

"Isn't that right, John?"

John nodded, even though he hadn't heard a word. "You're always right, Mother."

"See? That's why he's my favorite. Did you say Jonah was with his mother?"

Biting back an exasperated sigh, John shook his head. "His mother hasn't spoken to him in five years. I doubt he's with her today."

"What?" At Viv's screech, John blinked, wondering if he'd lost an eardrum. "What kind of woman doesn't talk to her own son, especially when she has one as sweet as Jonah?"

"Someone who hates gays, I suppose." Even to John's ears he sounded tired.

"Well," Viv said, sounding scandalized. She toyed with her purse straps, looking more pissed off by the second. He loved his mom. "As soon as my toes dry, we could always go kick her ass."

A smile touched John's lips before falling away. Within seconds, he was back to drowning. Jonah loved John's mom too, and everything was gone. Had Brad broken the news yet? Damn. This was hell and there was no end in sight.

FOUR

IT TURNED OUT TO BE EASIER THAN JONAH expected to walk away from college after years of hard work. He'd expected to feel like he'd let himself down or failed in some way. In truth, Jonah felt nothing at all. Maybe he was still numb from losing John. Perhaps he'd given his all and knew it. Whatever the reason, after leaving school and taking a long hot shower, Jonah didn't look back. That chapter of his life was now closed.

It was a nice night. He should go out. There wasn't a damn thing he wanted to do. Cricket's food bowl was still full from that morning. That was another thing he wasn't needed for, it seemed.

Jonah scooped up Cricket. "You didn't eat your food again. Look, buddy," he said, kissing his baby's head. "I know you miss Daddy. I do too, but you have to eat. We can't wither away." He curled up in the recliner with Cricket on his lap. Jonah ran his fingers through the dog's fur. "Besides, you still have me. I know I'm not much." Jonah's voice cracked on the admission. His throat swelled. Everything hurt. The silence was deafening. He couldn't recall the last time he'd felt so alone. At least when his friend Driver had lived across the street, he'd had someone to visit. Now there was no one. What had he done with his time before John?

"Are you tired of doggie food? Maybe I should get us something artery-clogging. You can't have chocolate, but you could have a little pizza." Jonah lifted Cricket so they could hold gazes. "Pizza never left anyone and never called again, right? I think we need a little of that in our lives. I'll run down to Sergio's and get us the good stuff. How's that sound?"

Any fucking thing sounded like a lifeline. The silence was crushing his eardrums. Jonah left Cricket in the recliner while he found some shoes and his wallet. He couldn't splurge forever. His savings account wouldn't hold out for long. Sooner or later, he'd need to find a real job. It wasn't that he was opposed to working. Jonah had always hoped to do something that fed his soul. He hadn't found that thing yet.

Jonah drove slow to Sergio's and took the long way. He didn't call ahead. There was no rush. Sitting inside the restaurant, waiting for his order, made him feel a little less alone. Maybe he'd stop at an actual movie rental place. They had one left in town. What did single people do? A wave of depression washed over Jonah. He'd learn. Since Jonah had zero desire to ever date again, he'd have to figure it out.

"Jonah Young."

At the sound of his name, Jonah pushed to his feet and made his way to the counter. Normally, the smell of pizza in the air would've been enough to rush him along. Tonight, he wasn't hungry. He was simply going through life's motions. Jonah drove home, taking the long way again. He was in no hurry to sit alone inside his house. In fact, he circled the block twice before convincing himself to pull into the driveway. It wasn't like there was anyone around to judge him.

As he came through the door, pizza in hand, he automatically used his feet to block Cricket from running out. The dog didn't meet him. He was still in Jonah's chair. Something wasn't right about that. After setting his haul on the coffee table, he checked on the dog. His breathing seemed shallow, and he didn't move.

Panic slammed into Jonah. He couldn't take another blow. When he lifted Cricket into his arms, the dog was limp like a rag doll. Jonah's heart raced.

"No, no, no. You're not allowed to leave me too," Jonah cried, racing for the door. Tears filled his eyes. There was an emergency vet a few blocks away. Jonah didn't know what else to do. He could barely breathe much less see straight enough to drive. Somehow, he still made it without killing anyone on the road. Jonah raced inside with Cricket held to his chest. A blonde woman working the front desk took one look at him and jumped to her feet, meeting Jonah halfway.

"I don't know what's wrong," he rambled, sounding panicked even to his ears. "He hasn't been eating, but I thought he was just depressed Now, he's not responding to anything."

"I've got him," she said, taking Cricket from his arms. "Kelly will have you fill out some paperwork, but I'll take him straight back."

Jonah nodded. "His name is Cricket." He didn't know why it mattered so much that she knew the dog's name. Maybe he hoped if she knew the dog's name, she'd realize Cricket was important to someone and do everything to help him.

Jonah filled out paperwork, barely comprehending anything he signed. His mind was with Cricket. Time passed like some sort of unreality. There was no one else there to witness him coming apart, giving Jonah the freedom to switch between pacing and sitting. He fought the urge to text John. It seemed like he should let John know, but Jonah worried it would seem like a ploy. John was done with him. He didn't care anymore what happened to Jonah, much less Jonah's dog. Jonah was alone. When a man wearing dark blue scrubs stepped into the waiting room, Jonah flew to his feet.

"Mr. Young?"

Jonah nodded. "It's Jonah. How is Cricket?"

Instead of answering, the man waved Jonah forward. "Follow me. I'll take you to see him. We can talk on the way."

With a nod, Jonah followed. As they cleared the doorway to the back, the man held out his hand. "I'm Dr. Perry, by the way."

Jonah accepted the man's handshake. His hand looked unnaturally pale in Dr. Perry's dark grip. "Thank you for caring for Cricket," Jonah said for lack of anything else.

"I've made him comfortable."

Against his will, Jonah's eyes fell closed at the words. He knew what they meant. Jonah had known from the moment he found Cricket lifeless that there wasn't any hope. That was how life went for him. When he lost, he lost everything. Life never half-ass fucked him. "Tell me." Even Jonah heard the dead note to his voice.

"Cricket has pancreatitis, which isn't uncommon for his breed. Usually, it's highly treatable, but in Cricket's case, it caused a blood clot that damaged his brain. He's having trouble breathing on his own. I'm so sorry."

"So he's suffering," Jonah surmised. He felt like he was the one dying. Jonah wondered if he could convince the doctor to put him out of his misery. It would be the kindest thing anyone could do for Jonah.

"I know a lot of people don't like to sit with their pets while they pass," the doctor said as he led Jonah into a room with Cricket.

Jonah couldn't look at the man. All he could see was his poor baby with an IV and oxygen, but still trying to get to Jonah. Jonah moved to Cricket's side and ran his fingers through the dog's fur. "I'll stay with him. It would break my heart twice as badly if I knew he was scared without me."

The doctor nodded. "I'll find you a chair."

Jonah didn't bother responding. He wasn't sure how a chair would make a damn bit of difference. Jonah blocked out the world and focused on Cricket. He rubbed the tiny dog's head and whispered his love. Jonah did and said whatever he could to make things easier. It was like watching the last piece of his life with John die. In a way, Cricket had been their baby. When it was done, Jonah just felt empty. He was completely alone in the world now. Nothing mattered anymore.

AFTER TWO HOURS IN BED, Jonah had given up on trying to sleep. Since then, he'd paced the floor, checked his bank balance, cried a little more, and checked the classifieds for job openings. He didn't need to make much to survive. With his house and car paid for, his expenses weren't high. It was odd how having a broken heart made everything else seem insurmountable. Paying Cricket's vet bill and final expenses had taken almost every cent Jonah had in savings. He might, if he stretched everything he had left, make it another two weeks without a job. Possibly he could start something minimum wage right away. Who knew? He wasn't good at anything. It was depressing as hell that he was almost twenty-four and had done nothing with his life. There was one option he couldn't avoid thinking about forever...

With his heart in his throat, Jonah logged into the sugar daddy's website. His biggest fear was seeing John back on the site as well. Everything had been bad enough lately. Jonah couldn't take the blow. He hovered over the "view profiles" option before chickening out and switching to the settings. He re-activated his profile and quickly closed the lid on his laptop. There. It was done. He took a deep breath. He'd let someone pick him from the site. If no one did, then he'd find another way to get the money to replace what he'd spent on Cricket's cremation. A lump formed in his throat. His phone buzzed across the desk, saving him from another round of tears. An unfamiliar number stared up at him from the face of the device.

555-5769: *This is Cricket's vet, Tyrone. I got your number from your file. I hope that's okay. This is a quick update on Cricket. He made it to the cremation center earlier. I took him over myself. I don't want to overstep any boundaries, but are you okay?*

A sad smile pulled at Jonah's lips. He hadn't known Dr. Perry's name was Tyrone. The man seemed nice—like he truly cared about animals. Jonah couldn't ignore him.

Jonah: *Thank you. I really appreciate the way you've gone above and beyond to care for Cricket's remains. Thank you for checking on me.*

After sending the message, he saved Tyrone's number as a new contact. He didn't know why. It simply gave him something to do with his hands. After hitting save, the phone buzzed again.

Tyrone: *I notice you avoided my question.*

Jonah pressed his lips together to keep from smiling. It seemed wrong for some reason.

Jonah: *Sorry. You probably don't want a genuine answer.*

Tyrone: *It sounds like you need coffee. There's a place close to my office. Coffee Sensation. I'm headed over there now. If you'd like, you can meet me there. If you're busy or don't show, I'll pretend I never asked.*

Confusion had Jonah's brows pulling together. He stared at his phone and chewed his bottom lip. No doubt, the guy was just being nice, but Jonah still didn't know how to react. Tyrone hadn't seen Jonah at his best. There was no way the man meant anything by the offer. Jonah glanced around. His house had never felt so empty. Fuck it. Jonah shoved his phone in his pocket and grabbed his keys. He couldn't sit here another second. Maybe Tyrone only meant to be nice and didn't really mean for Jonah to meet him, but Jonah had nothing else. It was a lifeline he couldn't ignore. Still, the short drive to Coffee Sensation left him a bundle of nerves. As he walked through the door, he was hyper aware that he looked a mess. His jeans were ripped in four places and his t-shirt had dried paint stains from his art class. Jonah was also fairly certain his hair stood in a few places. He hadn't even glanced in the mirror before leaving.

Jonah spotted Tyrone at a table in the back. He sipped at his coffee and stared down at his phone on the table. He wore the same style scrubs he had the night before. Unlike Jonah, he looked well rested and put together. Jonah paused at the edge of the table, unsure of what to say.

Tyrone glanced up. A welcoming smile stretched his lips. "You showed."

Jonah shifted from one foot to the other. "Hey."

"Hey," Tyrone said back, sounding sweet.

An odd desire to blush hit Jonah. He dropped his gaze to his hands as he pulled out the chair across from Tyrone and sat. It took every ounce of Jonah's will to meet Tyrone's gaze again. He cleared his throat. "So. How are you today?" Even to Jonah's ears, he sounded like he was simply making conversation.

"I'm okay." Tyrone's sweet brown gaze moved over Jonah's face. "How are you? Never mind. Don't answer that," Tyrone added just as quickly. "That's an unfair question today."

Jonah swallowed, wishing it was easier to breathe. "What are you drinking? It smells good." He was only making conversation. His heart hurt too badly to be uncomfortable, but he also didn't want to sit in silence.

"Toffee coffee. What can I order you?"

"I just came to keep you company. Since I haven't been to bed yet, I should probably skip the caffeine."

"You were really brave last night. A lot of people won't stay with their pets in their final moments. It's too hard. You were amazing."

Jonah's stomach hurt. His eyes burned. He didn't want to cry anymore. More than anything, he didn't want to lose anymore. He didn't know how to respond. "Maybe I'll take that coffee after all."

"Do you want it or are you searching for anything else to focus on?"

The question had Jonah blinking away the pain. His throat wouldn't work to answer.

Tyrone pushed to his feet. "Come on. If you're game, I'll show how I manage day in and day out, dealing with death."

Jonah stood. He didn't know Tyrone. It seemed a bit insane to go anywhere with the man. He wasn't worried. Anything was better than how he felt now, even turning up dead in a ditch.

THERE WERE no staples in his desk. It was such a small thing to set him off, but John fought the urge to put the stapler through the wall. All he needed was one goddamn staple. As much as he paid every fucking one who worked there, somebody could order the supplies needed. He stormed for the door.

"I'm going to the office supply store," he barked over his shoulder.

His receptionist scrambled after him. "Mr. Green, I'll go. Just tell me what you need."

He glared at her as he used his back to shove open the door. She backed away. An ounce of guilt tried worming its way in, but it wouldn't take. If he had to run his own goddamn errands, what was he paying other people to do? He fumed all the way to the store. There was a tiny voice in the back of his head, whispering he should just call Jonah. He should admit he made a bad decision and couldn't live without him. Whatever John had stolen from Jonah by standing in the way of his education, John could fix. By the time he made it to the supply store, John had talked himself into calling Jonah and back out of it again. Damned if he knew what the right thing to do was. He slammed the door on his SUV much harder than he intended.

"John?"

John glanced over his shoulder at the sound of his name. He caught sight of a familiar-looking guy. John couldn't place him. "Yeah."

The blond guy moved closer. John noticed his light hair was actually grayer than blond. There were also deep lines around his dark blue eyes. "It's Steve," he said, as if that cleared up the entire matter.

John blinked at him. "Okay."

"We used to work for competing medical supply companies."

Oh, Steve. Yeah, he remembered. They used to run into each other at least once a week at different doctor's offices. Damn. He looked old. John hoped he didn't look that old to other people. "How have you been?" John tried to sound like he wasn't as annoyed as he was. He didn't want to talk to anyone or make nice. John wanted to be alone if he couldn't be with Jonah.

"I'm good." His gaze slid down John's body. "You look amazing. I thought I'd heard you were working on some health food thing. You look the part."

Ha. He couldn't wait to tell Jonah. His brain froze. One day, that wouldn't be his first thought every time something happened. It seemed today wasn't that day. "Yeah. I'm helping to run my brother's company. It's done well for me. What about you? Are you still hitting up the doctors?"

Steve nodded. "It's what I'm good at, I suppose. What are you out doing now?"

John cast a glance toward the store. "Picking up some supplies."

"We should grab some lunch," Steve suggested. He bit his bottom lip as if he'd really put himself out there by asking. John hated to say no in the face of the guy's embarrassment. It wasn't like he had anything else going on.

"What did you have in mind?" Even John heard the reluctance in his tone. He smiled, trying to take the bite from his words. "The place next door looks dead," he added, motioning toward a steakhouse within walking distance. It was just lunch. He wasn't cheating on Jonah. Goddamn it.

Steve motioned toward the restaurant. "After you."

The instant his ass hit the seat inside the restaurant, John knew he'd made a mistake.

"John." The bellow had his head whipping around. David headed his way.

Fuck. "Mr. Baker. How are you?"

"Good. Good," he repeated. His gaze slid Steve's way. "Where's Jonah?"

Double fuck. David Baker was one of their biggest clients. As Hendrix had pointed out, David obviously liked Jonah. "School." John kept his voice firm, as if he really knew where Jonah was, and Jonah knew exactly where John was.

"Ah, that's too bad. I hate that I keep missing him. We were interrupted the last time we spoke. What did you say he studies at Stanford?"

"Engineering." John hoped by keeping his answers short, he could survive this conversation. He motioned toward Steve, not wanting to seem like he was hiding anything. "This is Steve. He's in sales too."

David cast a quick glance Steve's way, giving the man a nod before just as quickly dismissing him.

"Since I've missed him twice now, let's do dinner one night. I'd love to hear all about what Jonah plans to do with his degree."

John nodded. "We should do that. Let me talk it over with him and get back with you."

"Or we could hit that new place on the bluffs after the Blackwell charity event."

Fuck his life. He'd forgotten all about the upcoming event. "Maybe so. I'll let you know."

"I look forward to your call." With a final nod Steve's way, David headed for a nearby table where three other men sat, waiting.

"Is Jonah your son?"

John fought the urge to cover his face. Things weren't going his way. It was like Jonah was his good luck charm and he'd thrown the man away.

"Are you ready to order?"

He could've kissed the waitress for her good timing. He flipped up his menu, hiding from Steve. "This says something about your famous soup of the day. What is that?"

"You should probably stick with the salad. Soups have a lot of sodium," Steve pointed out.

John ground his back teeth. "So do dressings. I think I'll have the soup."

Steve shrugged. "Whatever. People like you keep people like me in business."

A pain bloomed behind John's eyes. An ache exploded through his chest. He missed Jonah. John missed ordering what he wanted and feeding his baby cake. "Maybe we should just order dessert and skip lunch."

A loud snort escaped Steve at the suggestion, but he didn't respond.

John set the menu aside and dug out his wallet. He didn't mind paying. In fact, if he could be with Jonah right then, he'd give any amount of money. John handed a fifty to the waitress. "For your trouble. Thank you." He set another on the table. "Please enjoy lunch on me. I just wanted one goddamn staple," he muttered under his breath as he slid from the booth. Without a backward glance, he headed for the door. Probably the guy thought he was an ass. Well, Steve would be right. He was the ass who'd ruined the only thing that mattered to him. Agreeing to lunch in the first place had been an insult to his heart. It was best he left a bad impression. That way, there was no chance of making the same mistake twice. It wasn't like he'd ever touch anyone else again anyhow. John's personal life was over.

DESPITE THE FACT that his life had been nothing but shit lately, Jonah couldn't stop smiling. The litter of puppies he'd just helped feed with medicine droppers were squirming all over him. They were so young, their eyes were still closed, and they were the most precious things he'd ever seen.

"You're smiling."

Jonah glanced up from the tiny brown balls of fur and met Tyrone's stare. "They're so cute."

"You're cute."

Heat exploded through Jonah's face. He glanced away.

"I didn't mean to embarrass you," Tyrone added.

Jonah shrugged. "You didn't. I just..." He shrugged again, uncomfortable.

Tyrone dropped to the floor next to Jonah. "I think you've found your calling. Have you ever thought about working with animals?"

Thankful for the subject change, Jonah met Tyrone's gaze again. He shrugged. "I've spent the last five years at Stanford, trying to get my engineering degree." He pulled a face. "I'm not sure more education is the answer for me."

"School isn't for everyone," Tyrone said, reaching

over and petting the tiny puppy Jonah held. "Not everything needs more education. Some things just need someone with heart."

Jonah worked up a genuine smile. He hadn't felt like he could talk to anyone in a long time. Tyrone felt like someone who would listen. "Thank you for this," he said, nodding toward the puppies. "Things have been really bad lately. Honestly, as much as I'm enjoying myself, I don't know how you do it. I don't think I could handle every day being like last night."

"Some days can seem pretty dark, but this is what I'm supposed to be doing. I truly believe that. I mean, think about it. What if when Cricket fell ill last night, I hadn't been here? What if you'd had nowhere to go? It wouldn't have changed anything. There was nothing that could be done, but you wouldn't have known that. Cricket would've passed at home and you would spend the rest of your life feeling like you didn't do all that could be done. I couldn't help him, but I was here, and I gave you that small peace. This job, it's hard some days, but it feeds my soul."

Jonah couldn't stop staring at Tyrone. He wanted to feel the way Tyrone did—like anything at all fed his soul. As stupid as most people would think it was, that was how Jonah had felt about being with

John. Every time he made John smile or eased his life in any way, it made him feel worthwhile—like he had purpose. He wasn't sure he'd ever feel that way about a job.

An embarrassed-looking smile touched Tyrone's lips. "I guess I sound crazy."

"No." Jonah set his hand on Tyrone's arm without thought. "You're amazing, and you're right. When I needed you, you were here. That matters."

Tyrone shifted just enough that Jonah found his hand inside Tyrone's. Tyrone's thumb lightly stroked him. "You look tired."

A snort escaped Jonah, and he rolled his eyes. "I'm not surprised."

"You're still gorgeous, though. I'm not sure you're capable of looking bad."

Jonah didn't know how to react. He was too tired to think on his feet. It seemed he should probably shut Tyrone down before the man got the wrong idea. Jonah wasn't sure he wanted to. "You'd be surprised."

"I'd like to find out."

The blush he'd been barely holding in exploded across his cheeks.

A sexy-sounding chuckle escaped Tyrone.

"Come on. I'll take you back to your car. You should probably try to get some sleep."

Jonah cast a longing glance toward the puppies. He didn't really want to go back to his empty house. "Okay."

"I would love it if you'd come back and help me out again," Tyrone said, obviously taking pity on him. "It'll be weeks before these little guys can leave here. Their mom didn't make it, so they need someone to feed them and cuddle them in her place."

"I'd love that." Even Jonah heard the smile in his voice.

Tyrone truly did have a sexy smile. "Let's get all these little guys back in the incubator." They worked side by side, loading all the puppies into the incubator, where they'd be warm. The next Tyrone spoke, he sounded unsure again. "I don't want to make you uncomfortable again, but maybe I can hang on to your number and text you again sometime."

Jonah glanced over. Tyrone was standing very close. He could see the gold specks in Tyrone's brown eyes. "I wouldn't be opposed to hearing from you again." He tried to sound unaffected.

Tyrone's smile said he failed. "Maybe I could also take you to dinner some night."

Jonah's phone buzzed before he could respond. He had a notification from the sugar daddy app. While keeping his phone tilted where Tyrone couldn't see, Jonah opened the app.

You have one offer.

Jonah clicked on the offer.

$500 for a black-tie event. Click Accept, Decline, or Counter-Offer.

His stomach churned as he hit accept. The smile pulling at Jonah's lips as he shoved his phone back in his pocket didn't match the trepidation in his heart. "Maybe I can take you to dinner instead?" He'd spent years as the one being cared for, and he'd been left behind. Jonah didn't relish the thought of being at anyone's mercy again. Maybe, for once, he'd be the one to spoil someone.

The surprise in Tyrone's expression made the impulsive offer worthwhile. "Go home. Get some sleep. Text me when you're up."

A hint of shyness had his gaze skirting away. "Okay." His gaze slid back Tyrone's way. There was confidence in the way Tyrone watched him. The saddest thought of all hit Jonah. It must be nice for someone to know their worth. If Tyrone never heard from Jonah again, he'd be fine. Just like everyone else on the planet.

FIVE

Dinner with Tyrone turned out to be one of the nicest meals Jonah had in ages. Tyrone asked questions and talked about his life. It was give and take. Jonah had forgotten how to hold a normal conversation. It had been so long since he'd had one.

After leaving the noisy wing bar, Jonah spotted a tiny ice cream shack by the ocean and pulled to the side of the road. A smile stretched his lips when Tyrone looked his way with his eyebrows raised in question. "When was the last time you had an actual ice cream cone?"

A sexy laugh caressed Jonah's ears. "You know, I don't remember. Maybe when I was a kid."

Jonah grabbed the door handle. "We should remedy that. What do you say?"

Tyrone's smile made the impulsive move worthwhile. "Sounds great."

They each chose a simple vanilla-chocolate swirl and headed for a bench facing the ocean. The breeze was nice, so was the view, but Tyrone's body held Jonah's attention. He looked good in jeans. Filled them out nicely. Jonah recognized he was trying harder than necessary to like Tyrone and forced his gaze away. Tyrone was nice, and he smelled good. Those things didn't make Jonah love John any less, and that shit was unfair. For several minutes, they sat in companionable silence, staring at the ocean.

Tyrone finally broke it. "You have me dying to know your whole story."

Jonah licked his ice cream before it dripped down the side of the cone. "What do you mean?"

A sexy-sounding chuckle escaped Tyrone, and he scooted closer. "I mean, you're young and gorgeous."

"Thank you," Jonah said with a laugh, interrupting.

Tyrone kept talking over him. "Your car is a Jag that can't be more than two years old. You own your own home. Most people I know my age can't afford that car and a house payment, but you do. All this while going to Stanford. Yet, you're unemployed. Do you come from money or sell drugs? What's your deal?"

Only the laughter in Tyrone's voice kept him from being offended. "To be fair, I quit Stanford. To answer your question though, I don't come from money. In fact, my father died in a car accident when I was three. I don't remember him at all. My mom never remarried and hasn't spoken a word to me in five years, so no help there." It was funny how he said the words so easily to Tyrone while John had been forced to drag the story from him. It seemed being the one who paid for dinner mattered after all. He didn't feel lacking in the least.

"So, it's drugs, then?"

A snort escaped Jonah before he could call it back. "No." He blew out a sigh. The last thing he wanted was for Tyrone to think badly of him, but he wasn't ashamed of loving John. "Have you ever heard of Green's Fighter Fuel?"

Tyrone nodded. "I have some of their meals in my freezer."

Jonah took another bite of his ice cream before plunging in with both feet. It was best for him to learn now if Tyrone would think he was a gold digger and run away. "I just got out of a three-year-long relationship with one of the owners, John Green."

"Wow."

"Yeah," Jonah said, matching Tyrone's tone.

Tyrone kicked his feet up on the railing separating the bench from the beach. He draped his arm across the bench behind Jonah. "So... what I'm hearing is, you like older men."

A loud laugh burst from Jonah, forcing him to cover his mouth.

Tyrone didn't let up. "Because, you know, I'm older and available." That was true. Tyrone was older, but not by much. By Jonah's best guess, Tyrone was in his early thirties. The other half of Tyrone's claim still didn't make sense to Jonah. He had to know.

"Why are you single?" Jonah asked, since Tyrone had opened the door. Jonah kicked through it like a cop on a drug raid. "You're sexy and successful. It doesn't make sense that someone hasn't already snatched you up."

"Honestly?"

"Of course."

"I'm a workaholic," Tyrone said, as if admitting a dirty secret. "It's rare for me to not be on call. I'm passionate about what I do, and I haven't met anyone who tolerates being second for long."

A snort escaped Jonah. He tossed his unfinished ice cream in a trash can a foot away and swiped his fingers on his pants. "Hell, I'd settle for being fifth at this point." Jonah pressed his lips together. No one could've been more shocked by the sudden confession than him. He loved John, and he'd been happy, but now that John was gone, Jonah realized John hadn't been perfect. He pushed John from his mind. Jonah was here with Tyrone. John didn't want him. Not anymore. Tyrone's silence cut through Jonah's thoughts. He turned his head and found the man staring at him as if waiting to have Jonah's attention. He was closer than Jonah realized. Their faces were only inches apart.

"From what I've seen of you so far, you're pretty damn amazing." Tyrone moved closer. Jonah did too. As Jonah looked on, Tyrone's eyes fell closed. Their lips brushed. Jonah's heart skipped a beat.

Tyrone's phone buzzed, and he leaned away with a growl. He checked the face. "See what I mean? A dog was just brought in from being hit by a car. I have to go."

Jonah stood. "Do you need any help?"

Tyrone's gaze moved over his features. "Are you up for that? It might not end well."

"If that's the case, then I'd hate for someone's pet to pass alone."

A sweet smile touched Tyrone's lips. "You know, I think I could use an assistant."

Jonah motioned toward the car. "As it happens, I'm free." It probably said something terrible about him that Jonah couldn't think of anything he'd rather be doing than heading toward an animal ER. That wasn't one hundred percent true. There was one thing he'd rather be doing, but those days were gone. Jonah had to find something new to love before life killed him.

JOHN BANGED on Jude's door then shushed himself. "*Shhh*. Your brother has neighbors."

"What the fuck?" Jude said, throwing open the door. He looked ready to tear apart whoever was pounding on his door in the middle of the night. His face cleared when he spotted John. "What's wrong?"

"I'm a stupid, stupid man." Even John heard the slur in his voice.

"Are you drunk?"

"Don't leave him standing on the porch," Hendrix said behind Jude.

John squinted, trying to see Hendrix. He could hear him but not see him. "There's my brother-in-law. He knows. From the first time he set eyes on me, he knew I'm a stupid man." Even John recognized he was repeating himself. He couldn't stop.

Jude released a loud sigh. "Oh, for fuck's sake. Come in."

John tripped coming through the door. He quickly righted himself. "You have a little step up there I've never noticed."

"Yes. It's the floor's fault." John ignored Jude's dry tone. Jude steered him toward the couch. "Would you like to tell me what's going on?"

"I'll put some coffee on," Hendrix said, leaving them alone.

John fell across the couch and covered his eyes with his arm. "I'm a stupid man."

"We've established you're stupid. Can you expound a bit?"

"I broke things off with Jonah."

"Oh. Why?"

A shot of outrage had John uncovering his eyes to glare at Jude. "I ruined my life and all you have is oh?"

Jude sat on the coffee table and shrugged. "You've already covered being dumb. What else do you want me to say?"

John re-covered his eyes. "I don't know."

Another loud sigh sounded through the room. "Do you plan to tell me what happened?"

"I'm s—"

"I swear by all that's holy if you say you're stupid one more time instead of answering me, I will punch the stupid right out of you."

Once again, John uncovered his eyes, this time only long enough for Jude to see him rolling them. "I was going to say I'm selfish and spoiled."

"You're still not telling me anything new here."

"It was new to me." Even John heard the petulance in his tone. "Jonah isn't graduating because of me. I also had no idea his shitty fucking mom hasn't spoken to him in five years. What kind of person doesn't know either of those things about someone they've been with for years? Me. The idiot," John said, stabbing himself in the chest with his thumb. "That's who."

"I don't see how either of those things are on you."

John quickly sat up. A little too quickly. He cupped his head between his knees when the room

73

spun. "I never asked questions." The wind had gone out his sails, and he sounded tired. "If I'd asked questions, instead of always talking about myself, I would've known I made him miss too many days of school. I would've noticed he'd never introduced me to his family."

"Okay. It does seem you should've noticed you hadn't met his family. But I don't think the failing school is on you. I mean, you paid for his college, right?"

"Probably."

"Jesus Christ, John. You don't even know if you paid for his school." Judging by Jude's tone, he was finally getting it.

John shrugged. "Bills came in. I paid them."

A cup appeared beneath his nose. "Drink this."

John accepted the coffee from Hendrix. He sat back as Hendrix filled the spot next to Jude on the coffee table. They both stared at him expectedly.

"Am I a bad person?"

"You're one of the best people I know," Jude said, sounding sincere. "It's possible you mistook giving gifts as showing attention, but Jonah has always seemed happy to me. What did he say about all this?"

John shrugged. "Brad handled it."

Jude blinked. "You had your lawyer dump him."

Even though Jude's words had obviously been a statement, John still nodded.

"Well, now you're a bad person," Hendrix said while patting John's knee, as if that softened the blow.

John deflated. "I don't know what to do."

"Oh, you'll have to grovel."

Jude nodded, completely aligned with his husband. "A lot. Like you've never scraped and begged before in your life."

John rubbed his chest. "The thing is, I'm not sure he isn't better off without me."

"So, you what?" Jude asked with a shrug. "You plan to stay drunk and pity party on my couch?"

"I didn't say *I* was better off."

"Lord, Jesus," Hendrix muttered, coming to his feet. "I'm going back to bed."

Jude grabbed Hendrix's hand before he could get away and hauled him in for a kiss. "I'll be there in a little while, baby."

John couldn't look. He missed being happy too much. When Hendrix left them alone, Jude moved to the couch beside him and draped his arm over John's shoulders. "I know you'll do the right thing. You always do in the end."

"I don't want to do the right thing. I want to be with Jonah."

"There you go, then," Jude said, making it sound so simple. "Love is never the wrong answer."

John wasn't so sure that was true. His love had suffocated Jonah, stealing his life. Maybe John didn't know how to love anyone the right way. Maybe he was broken.

SIX

JONAH NEVER WOULD'VE BELIEVED A KNOCK ON his front door could instill so much suspicion in him. He creeped toward the door, wishing he had a baseball bat or anything. There was no one who would come see him any longer. He opened the door a crack. Happiness exploded through him and Jonah threw the door wide.

"Driver!"

While wearing a bright smile, Driver pulled open the screen door and led his dog Sam inside. Driver had lived across the street from Jonah for months before marrying the only person to ever steal his heart. Jonah was happy for him, but he also missed Driver like crazy.

"Hey, babe. We had to come check on the house

since we have a tenant moving in at the end of the week. Sam saw your house and went crazy. There was no way he was leaving without seeing you."

"I'm so glad you made Daddy stay long enough to see me. I've missed you both so much." He gave Sam a huge hug before letting him run free through the house. "Where's Cortland?" Jonah asked as he came to his feet.

"He had to..." Driver's gaze moved over Jonah's shoulder. "Go put that back."

Jonah turned to find Sam dragging Cricket's doggie bed into the living room. "Oh, buddy. I'm sorry." Jonah moved to retrieve the large weighted pillow Cricket had used as a bed from Sam. He rubbed the dog's head as he tossed the pillow back into the kitchen. "Cricket is gone, baby." His voice cracked. He swallowed, but no more words would come. Even Jonah realized he looked like he was drowning on dry land.

Driver moved closer. "What happened?"

Jonah swallowed again. He kept his gaze averted until the burning behind his eyes and nose subsided. "The vet said pancreatitis. A clot formed and went to his brain before anyone could do anything."

To his surprise, Driver rubbed his back. "I'm so sorry. You should've called. Cortland and I would've been here in a heartbeat." The large former soldier had a lot of dark points. Jonah understood that Driver had some mental problems, but he'd always really liked Driver. Since meeting the man's husband, Cortland, Jonah had found another good friend.

"I'm just, you know..." Jonah waved his hands, searching for a way to explain. "I guess I'm just private, or maybe I think I over burden people. Hell, I don't know. It's like, no one likes a negative person and people already don't like me for me, so I suffer in silence," Jonah finished lamely. He didn't know how to explain how he felt like no one cared enough to be bothered with him.

"Pack a bag and come home with us."

A smile briefly passed over Jonah's lips at the offer. "I can't. I accepted a date for tonight that I can't afford to miss. Cricket's final vet bill and expenses crippled me."

Driver swiped his hand through the air. "Wait. I can't believe John didn't pay for all that. He's never hesitated to cover things in the past. I mean, I would think you'd have to stop him from building a freaking monument in Cricket's honor in the front yard."

Despite the pains in his chest, a chuckle fell from Jonah's lips. He could see John doing exactly that.

"John is gone too." Jonah's gaze hit the floor as the confession landed. He cleared his throat. "Um, I guess he got tired of me."

"Wow. I..." Driver blinked. He looked like words failed him.

A smile he didn't feel touched Jonah's lips. He turned away and went down on his haunches to love on Sam. "It's okay." Even to Jonah's ears, the claim sounded like a lie. "This date tonight pays enough to last me a couple of weeks. Hopefully, I'll find a job before the money runs out. It's just, whatever, right?" The gigantic German shepherd, golden retriever mix did his best to hug Jonah back, eating up all the attention. Jonah kissed the dog's head. "Maybe I'll just give up on people."

"Don't go tonight," Driver burst out, taking Jonah by surprise with the worry lacing every word. "Pack a bag and come home with us. No one can spend five minutes in Wyld's company without smiling. Cortland and I will pay for Cricket's final expenses. Anything could happen to you with a stranger."

The obvious concern in Driver's voice warmed Jonah's heart, but Jonah had to take care of himself. He had to stop letting everyone else carry him because—eventually—everyone else left. "I love you for offering, but I don't want to spend the night as the fifth wheel. I don't think I can swallow anyone else's happiness right now. No offense."

Driver's intense blue gaze screamed worry, but he nodded. "I understand. At least keep your phone handy so you can call me if you feel uncomfortable."

Jonah sat and let the huge dog crawl into his lap. "I will," he promised. "This is just something I have to do, but I do appreciate your friendship." He did. Jonah recognized he was lucky to have someone like Driver he could call. But he wouldn't. Even if he ended up on a date with the devil himself, Jonah already knew he wouldn't ask for help. He simply didn't know how to reach for any life preserver. Jonah imagined, someday soon, life would finally drown him, and he would float away.

THE BAD FEELING in Jonah's gut wouldn't subside. From the moment Jonah answered the door, he wished he hadn't accepted this gig. His date for the black-tie event was probably fifty and balding. His looks had nothing to do with Jonah's discomfort. It was the way Wayne looked at him—like sizing up cattle. Cattle he planned to fuck. That wasn't happening.

On the way to the car, Wayne hit strike two in Jonah's books. "Your house is inconveniently located. Next time, I'll have you meet me."

Jonah flashed Wayne a sweet smile while mentally flipping him the bird. The guy was insane if he thought there'd be a next time.

"At least you know how to dress."

There was that. His tux was one of John's many purchases for Jonah. It cost more than Wayne's car, which wasn't that great for such a pompous ass.

"I assume, since you're dressed appropriately, that you've attended events like this one."

"Yes." Jonah kept his voice bland but polite. All he wanted was to make it through the night. "In fact, I attended this event last year."

Wayne's head whipped around. "I don't want people knowing I've paid you to accompany me."

"They won't," Jonah assured him. "I said I've been. Not that I was paid to attend. You have nothing to worry about."

Wayne's hackles lowered. "Oh. Okay. That's good." Wayne set his hand on Jonah's knee. All the alarm bells clanged. They were in a car. Wayne didn't have to go where he claimed they were headed. For a moment, Jonah floundered before finally deciding to leave it. As long as it didn't go higher, and the man didn't make any unexpected stops, he'd ignore the touching for now.

By the time they made it to the hotel hosting the charity event, Jonah's stomach was in knots. He was hyper aware of every breath he took and Wayne's hand on his skin. Jonah worried his nerves would snap at any moment. He wasn't used to being touched without his permission. Each breath he took felt like it came through a straw.

Jonah concentrated on his surroundings as they cleared the door. Wayne's palm kept colliding with the small of Jonah's back. His touch wasn't comfortable. It was possessive. Jonah wished it would stop. With a bland smile in place, he eyed the gorgeous crystal light fixtures and admired the flower arrangements brought in for the event. Jonah concentrated on anything and everything that wasn't Wayne.

"Jonah?"

Jonah spun at the sound of his name. The first genuine smile of the night pulled at the corners of his mouth. "Mr. Baker. It's so good to see you."

David held both hands out to Jonah. Jonah didn't hesitate to accept. "Please, Jonah. How many times do I have to tell you? It's just David." He kissed Jonah's cheek before releasing him. Jonah could feel Wayne's displeasure at his back.

"One more time, I suppose." Jonah always answered David the same because it made the man laugh. He'd always had a special fondness for David Baker. The man had kind eyes. They were a blue that reminded Jonah of the water in the Florida Keys. He was a hair older than John and graying at the temples. For some reason Jonah couldn't explain, David always made him wish he had a dad like him.

"I've missed you the last few times I've seen John."

Jonah fought the urge to wince. "I've been busy with school."

"Don't forget who you came here with," Wayne said close to Jonah's ear.

David's eyes flashed with annoyance in Wayne's direction. "Is there some reason you feel the need to interrupt us?"

Jonah bit the inside of his cheek to keep from smiling. Everyone respected David. He sat on every board and had a finger in every pie.

Wayne didn't exactly bow under the pressure of David's scathing stare, but he went away. "I need a drink," he muttered, heading for the bar.

David shook his head as he watched Wayne go. "What was John thinking, leaving you alone in this crowd? There are so many blackguards waiting around every corner."

Jonah couldn't fight his smile a second longer. Who even said blackguard anymore? "I'm pretty good at taking care of myself."

"But you shouldn't have to," David said, sounding one hundred percent honest. "There's a big difference between John and the rest of the old perverts around here. He loves you. The rest of these men think they're owed any man they want." David added a sharp nod like he was the expert on the matter. Jonah tried breathing past the hurt. John didn't love him. No one did, but it was kind of sweet that David believed. Sooner or later, he'd have to admit he'd been dumped. Right now, he didn't have the heart.

Someone called David's name. He flashed a blatantly false smile in that direction before focusing on Jonah once more. His smile turned genuine again. "The wolves have found me," he said, sounding scandalized. "If I see John, I'll be sure to send him to your side. We must make dinner plans."

Jonah nodded. "Agreed."

With a final wave, David headed in the opposite

direction, leaving Jonah alone in the crowd. He tried taking a deep breath to calm his nerves. Hopefully, John wasn't actually there. What a nightmare that would be. He shouldn't have accepted this date. It was a mistake. A weight sat on his gut. Something bad would happen if he stayed, even if John wasn't there. Wayne struck Jonah as mean while sober, and he'd gone to the bar. He cast a glance in that direction.

Wayne appeared from nowhere. "I brought you a glass of champagne."

A glass that had been in Wayne's possession long enough to slip anything inside. Jonah didn't reach for it. "Thank you, but I don't drink."

Wayne's smile tightened. "You're about to start."

Jonah hardened his voice. "No. I'm not."

"I think you forget who owns you tonight."

There it was, the ugliness he'd been waiting on. "Me. That's who owns me. Have a great night," Jonah said, giving Wayne a sharp nod. He made it two steps before Wayne grabbed his arm and squeezed—hard enough to leave bruises. "You're not going anywhere. I've already paid your fee."

Jonah spun and went flush against Wayne, hiding his actions from the room. He grabbed Wayne by the balls and squeezed. "Don't you ever touch me again." Wayne whimpered. Jonah didn't let up. He'd not gone into this business lightly. No one touched him without his permission. "I'll make sure your fee is returned, but if you ever put your hands on me again, you'll lose this permanently. Understood?" Without waiting for an answer, Jonah walked away. He was enraged. Not just with Wayne but with life in general. He always tried to be the best person he could be, and still everything slipped through his fingers. In the last few weeks, he'd lost everything he loved. Jonah was beyond tired and heartsick. Being manhandled by a pervert was the straw that broke him. His deal with John had never made him feel cheap. Jonah didn't know what he'd expected from tonight. He hadn't found it.

As he hit the sidewalk and dragged the night air into his lungs, Jonah pulled out his phone. Hopefully, he wouldn't have to wait long for a ride share or cab. The last thing he wanted was to go another round with rapey Wayne should he decide to follow. A solid weight landed on Jonah's shoulders as he pulled up the app to hire a car. He shrugged the hands from his shoulders and spun. "Look, I've already warned you—" The words died on his lips at the sight of the most beautiful man he'd ever met. "John. Sorry, I..." John's pinched expression sank in.

Jonah's heart skipped a beat. "Oh, sweetie. Are you okay? You're not," he said before John could answer. Jonah knew that look. Granted, he hadn't seen it in over a year. He'd thought John's doctor had finally gotten John's headaches under control, as long as John avoided alcohol.

The valet appeared before John spoke a word. "Your vehicle, Mr. Green."

"Thank you," Jonah said, snagging the keys before John could. He dug some money from his wallet and tipped the man, ignoring John's attempts at stopping him. When John tried shoving his money aside, Jonah grabbed his hand and held on. "Come on, baby. I'll take care of everything." To his surprise, John let Jonah lead him to the passenger side of the massive SUV and dutifully climbed inside when Jonah opened the door. Jonah didn't stop there. He couldn't let John slip into a full-blown migraine or the pain would have him down for a week. Too many people depended on John. He buckled John's seatbelt, and while perched on the edge of John's seat, he dug through the console for his meds. When he found the prescription bottle, he shook out two pills and passed them John's way. "I'll run through the closest drive-thru and get you a drink."

"Thank you."

Jonah finally stopped fussing long enough to meet John's gaze. He looked sad. The idea of John not being the shiniest star in every room hurt Jonah's chest. "You never have to thank me." He stopped there because he had too much to say and most of it Jonah wanted to say in anger. Like how he'd thought they were friends, contract or not. He'd never in a million years dreamed there would come a day John wouldn't call him again, and then that day had come. Jonah blinked and turned away before John saw the instant tears. No one had ever cut him deeper. Jonah had no one else to blame but himself.

He tried closing the door as softly as possible so he wouldn't make John's headache worse. Once he climbed behind the wheel, Jonah turned off the radio. He reached for John's hand. John didn't fight him. The way he let Jonah care for him let Jonah know exactly how bad he felt. John was the caretaker. Everyone's caretaker. He always drove, paid, made the first move, and the last. Yet he sat in silence as Jonah bought him a drink. Granted it was a dollar soda from a fast-food joint, but it was the first time.

"I'm taking you home with me." Jonah didn't ask. He simply pointed the car in that direction. If John passed out, there was no way Jonah could get him up three flights of stairs to his bedroom. Jonah's place was smaller. He could take better care of him in his own space.

John never said a word. Still, Jonah breathed a sigh of relief when they reached his house. He didn't want to fight. Between getting treated like a whore and everything else he'd endured lately, Jonah didn't have a nerve left to spare. Inside the door, John toed off his shoes alongside Jonah. They both peeled off their jackets and ties. Jonah's heart turned over in his chest. He missed this. It was such a small thing to stab him in the chest, but Jonah missed every teeny tiny detail of them.

"Do you need anything?"

"No."

John's answer sounded gruff. Jonah tried not to read anything into it. The man's head hurt. He led John to the couch. The moment Jonah kicked back in the recliner, he patted his lap. "Head here."

John's gaze stayed locked on his as curled onto his side facing Jonah and set his head on Jonah's lap. Jonah ran his hand through John's soft locks and massaged his temple. John's eyelids drooped a little more by the second. His breathing deepened. Even once John dozed off, Jonah didn't stop stroking the man's hair. Maybe John didn't love him. Possibly he never would. The knowledge changed nothing. Jonah loved him. The giant ass.

JOHN CAME AWAKE WITH A START. His heart raced into his throat at the unfamiliar surroundings until his gaze landed on Jonah. He was sound asleep with his fingers in John's hair. Jonah was beautiful in a way John had never encountered anywhere else. He'd been out with someone else. A pain exploded behind his eyes again at the memory of watching Jonah go flush against another man before walking away. The idea of Jonah with anyone else sat heavy on John's chest. He'd hope Jonah wouldn't need to find another old man to care for him with the severance package he'd offered. Of course, the stubborn ass had refused to accept anything. The concern etched on Jonah's face when he'd realized John was in pain wouldn't leave John's head. Jonah owed him nothing. If anything, John was the one in his debt because Jonah had given up everything in the past three years to keep John happy. Yet Jonah hadn't turned his back on John. It was almost like Jonah loved him.

As much as John wished he could stare at Jonah

all night, getting older sucked and his bladder was ready to burst. While trying his damnedest not to wake Jonah, John rolled from the couch and padded toward the bathroom. When he caught sight of himself in the mirror, John froze. There were dark circles under his eyes and the WTF lines between his eyes looked deeper than usual.

"Jesus," he muttered, turning away and heading for the toilet. Jonah shouldn't want to be seen with him. He looked old as hell. As John washed his hands, he decided he would leave. Jonah deserved a chance to spend time with people his own age. The moment he stepped outside the bathroom, his gaze landed on Cricket's doggie bed. A smile pulled at his lips. When he'd bought the tiny Miniature Schnauzer for Jonah, Jonah had never looked happier. Love had etched his features the moment he set eyes on the dog. Then Cricket had barked, sounding dead up like a cricket's chirp, and the poor little guy hadn't stood a chance at landing a manly name.

John glanced around. Cricket was nowhere to be seen. He searched every room, finally wandering into Jonah's bedroom. He'd intentionally saved that room for last. It smelled too much like Jonah's sexy skin. The scent permeated every inch. There still wasn't any sign of the dog. Jonah's dresser caught his attention. One half of the mirror was covered in pictures. John moved closer. Three stuffed animals he'd bought Jonah sat beneath the pictures. John smiled at the sight. Then he leaned closer to the images and his breath disappeared. Picture after picture of them outlined their time together. Jonah looked happy. Genuinely happy. In each picture, he smiled bright on the verge of laughter. John looked even happier than Jonah. He didn't recognize that version of himself any longer. John couldn't remember the last time he'd smiled and meant it. Losing Jonah had killed everything good.

"How's your head?"

John startled at the question. His heart beat fast enough to jump from his chest. He took a breath, trying to calm the racing before turning Jonah's way. "I was looking for Cricket," he said instead of answering, hoping Jonah wouldn't think he'd been snooping.

A deep line appeared between Jonah's eyes. He visibly swallowed and looked away. "He died."

Horror overcame John at the pain in Jonah's voice. "Oh no. What happened? You should've called. I would've been here for you."

Jonah continued staring at the wall as if he

couldn't meet John's stare. He toyed with the trim around the doorframe. "Would you? I'm not so sure."

John wanted to be angry. In fact, his first reaction was a shot of outrage. It died as quickly as it hit. He hadn't given Jonah a reason to believe in him lately. John closed the distance between them. He snagged Jonah around the waist. "Come here, baby. I'm so sorry. I know how much you love him. Is there anything I can do?"

Jonah shook his head as John towed Jonah against his chest. "The vet has someone they use for cremation. They'll return the ashes to me later."

"You shouldn't have had to go through all that alone."

"No one gave me a choice," he said against John's chest. Jonah pushed away and swiped at his eyes while avoiding John's gaze. "You didn't answer my question. How's your head?"

It was obvious Jonah was hurting, but he wouldn't accept John's comfort. John had no one to blame but himself. He'd cut all ties to Jonah. John couldn't speak. His throat hurt too badly.

Jonah finally met his gaze. He looked how John felt. A loud sigh fell from Jonah's lips, sounding like it came from the man's soul. "Come here," he said, sounding tired as he reached for John's shirt. Jonah watched his hands as he unbuttoned John's shirt and shoved the material down John's arms. "Let's go to bed. If you're not answering me, that means you're still hurting, and you don't want to admit it because you don't want me to take care of you." With John's shirt held against his chest, Jonah moved to the bed and angrily jerked back the covers. "But that's just too damn bad. I know I'm not who you want anymore, but I'm who you got tonight, so get in the goddamn bed."

John held his tongue and stripped off his pants. He didn't tear his gaze away from Jonah for a single second as Jonah did the same. The instant they were beneath the covers, John snagged Jonah around the middle and hauled the man against him. "You're the only one I'll ever want," he confessed against Jonah's skin as he kissed him beneath the ear.

Jonah took a ragged-sounding breath. "I think I fucking hate you." Jonah's confession came out so quietly John questioned if he'd heard him at all, except it also sounded like a fucking cannon to John's heart. Jonah rolled in his arms. After snaking his leg over John's hips, Jonah pulled him in for a kiss. He didn't toy with John, making him question where this was headed. "I'm so goddamn mad at you," Jonah said before deepening their kiss. Jonah nipped at his lips and sucked on his tongue while his fingers found their way inside John's underwear. He had John questioning his ability to last as he ruthlessly stroked John's cock. There could be no doubt Jonah wanted him. This wasn't a business transaction. There was no contract, obligating Jonah's availability. This was Jonah taking what he wanted. He'd chosen the right man.

John rolled Jonah beneath him and tore at what was left of their clothes. He kissed and bit his way down Jonah's body, needing all the moans he'd been missing since walking away. Jonah pulled at his hair and clawed at his skin. As Jonah's cock hit the back of John's throat, the discovery that had been creeping its way in landed on John like a lead weight. They'd never been only a business arrangement. Jonah cared about him. John hadn't accomplished anything by walking away from Jonah. He'd been stupid. John had broken both their hearts. He'd thought he was doing the right thing by Jonah. Now he realized all he'd done was fail them. All he'd done was break something beautiful. He'd make it right.

Jonah dug his heels into the mattress and lifted his hips. He was wild beneath John, seeking release. There were things no one could fake. Jonah's desperation to have him was one of those things.

John's heart couldn't take another second of not being inside Jonah. He'd thought it wouldn't happen again. Now, here they were. John crawled up Jonah's body. His whimpers assaulted John's ears. John would fix it.

"Please tell me there are still condoms here." Even John heard the growl in his voice. He didn't wait for an answer before tearing open the bedside table and digging for what he needed. John was rougher than he intended as he lubed Jonah's ass. He tried to move slower. His mind was too big of a mess. They needed to be one. The second he was suited up, John snagged Jonah's hips, shoved Jonah's knee higher, and pushed his way inside. Jonah gasped as his body made room for him.

John froze and pressed his forehead to Jonah's chest. The madness inside him had his heartbeat pounding in his ears. He felt the rapid beating of Jonah's heart kissing his forehead. Everything slowed. He reached between them and massaged Jonah's cock. At first, he kept his touch light, trying to slow things down. Jonah's tight ass squeezed John's dick, trying to suck him deeper. John gasped for air. The light pouring from the open bathroom doorway illuminated Jonah's skin. John stayed buried deep, letting Jonah's body milk him while he watched

Jonah's cock disappear inside his closed hand, over and over again. Jonah writhed. John pumped faster. He could feel Jonah's body winding tighter by the second. He stiffened beneath John. At the first twitch, he aimed for his mouth, needing to catch the cum on his tongue. Between the salty flavor and the suction on his cock, a wave of ecstasy crashed over John. He slowly rolled his hips, riding out each wave. As he pumped the condom full, John wished there was nothing between them. He wished this was their bed and Jonah had his last name. John never wanted to question where he stood, and he wanted Jonah to know he always came first. He needed Jonah to understand he was loved.

As he claimed Jonah's lips, John swore to himself he'd find a way. All those things would be just like any other idea he had. Once it took hold, nothing would stop him from achieving every goal he set. Jonah would be his again. This time, it would be for good. If Jonah gave him another chance, John would never fail him again.

SEVEN

From his spot on the bed, Jonah watched John move silently through the room, gathering his clothes. His heart ached. Jonah's throat burned with unspoken words. He wanted to pour his heart out and beg John to stay. At least, part of him did. The rest of Jonah hadn't forgotten what it was like to be abandoned. The anger that built while trapped inside silence was choking. Jonah had experienced the sensation too many times in one lifetime. The helpless frustration of having someone he loved turn their back on him lived in Jonah's soul. For the rest of his life, he would suffer through it over the loss of his mother. Then, John had done the same. Jonah's entire body felt heavy with exhaustion from trying to hold on to people who pushed him away.

After buttoning his shirt, John sat on the edge of the bed. He caressed Jonah's hip, urging him onto his back. "I hate leaving when you're still curled up, looking warm and waiting."

Without thought, Jonah's palm slid across John's hard stomach. He fought the urge to lure John back to bed. Instead, he set John free, because the man didn't belong to him. Not anymore. "It's okay. I know you can't stay."

"If I could cancel my morning meeting, I would. I'd rather be here."

Jonah refused to search the words for lies. His heart was already broken. There was nothing left for John to break. "Don't think about it." Jonah didn't know who the words were meant to soothe, John or himself.

John's lips found his. Jonah let it happen. He was greedy like that. It seemed there would never come a time when Jonah had enough of John's kisses. No matter the cost. "Go back to sleep, sexy," John whispered against his lips. "We'll be together again before you have time to miss me."

It was too late. Jonah already knew his loss. He kept the words to himself and savored John's kiss. It was over too soon. Even after John disappeared from the room, Jonah couldn't stop staring at the door that had stolen him. For hours, he stayed in bed, refusing to think. He had the rest of his life to regret another night. Solitude would storm his life again without permission soon enough.

When the silence pressed on his eardrums with enough force to make them ring, Jonah rolled from the bed. He carefully kept his mind blank as he moved through his usual morning routine. No matter how hot he turned the water, his shower still felt cold. His mind shied away from the reason. He refused to linger over the knowledge he'd lost John all over again. It was impossible to lose what he never had. Jonah dressed and put on his shoes. He didn't bother eating. Food no longer held any appeal. With phone in hand, he opened the door, leaving the scent of John's cologne behind.

Jonah drew up short. Brad stood with his hand raised as if ready to knock. For a moment, Jonah blinked at the lawyer in surprise.

"Um, good morning."

Brad smiled, looking every bit as shocked as Jonah felt. He dropped his hand. "Good morning. John sent me to pick you up."

"Why?" Even Jonah heard the annoyance in his voice, but really. John disappeared and then expected Jonah to jump when called. It wasn't happening.

"He'd like to go over a new contract with you."

Jonah stepped out, forcing Brad to take a step back or get hit with the screen door. He pulled the front door closed behind him. "No thanks."

Brad visibly floundered. "What do you mean no thanks?"

"Just what I said. I'm not interested in a new contract. Now, if you'll excuse me, I have somewhere to be."

Brad followed closely on Jonah's heels all the way to the car. "Why are you wearing scrubs?"

A loud sigh choked Jonah. "I'm volunteering at a veterinarian's office. They gave me scrubs so I wouldn't ruin any more clothes. God knows I can't afford them," Jonah muttered as he opened his car door.

"I think you should hear John out."

An unexpected smile pulled at Jonah's lips as he focused on Brad once more. "I've spent a lot of time listening to John. Now I have something else to do."

"What should I tell John?"

Jonah paused with one foot inside the car. "Whatever you want, I suppose."

"I don't mean to push," Brad said in a rush,

stopping Jonah from getting away. "You love him. Everyone sees that."

A sad smile pulled at his lips. "I don't want to be in love alone anymore. John spent three years with me and doesn't know me at all. Hell, maybe I don't know me either." Without giving Brad a chance to argue further, Jonah slid behind the wheel. He gave the man a tiny wave as he backed from the driveway. Jonah wasn't angry. He didn't want to be a dick. All Jonah wanted was to be loved as fiercely as he'd loved John. He didn't think it was too much to ask. If all John wanted was another contractual agreement, maybe Jonah wasn't the one for him after all.

THE GLASS DOORS leading into John's office weren't transparent enough to satisfy John's impatience to see Jonah. Spending the night holding Jonah hadn't soothed his need for the other half of his soul in the least. The sickening hollow sensation in his gut grew with every second that passed without Jonah. He'd barely made it through his morning meeting. John's long-time lawyer, Brad, made his way down the hall. He was alone. John's heart beat faster the closer Brad came. Their gazes met as Brad pulled open the door and John knew. Jonah wasn't coming.

The well-dressed lawyer looked nervous as he crossed the room. "He said no thanks," Brad said, putting John out of his misery.

"No thanks," John repeated. Even he heard the confusion in his voice.

Brad nodded. "He said he wasn't interested in another contract."

"And?"

Brad shrugged. "And nothing. He was dressed in scrubs and on his way out when I got there. I thought he'd found some sort of hospital job, but it seems he's volunteering at a veterinarian's office."

"Really?" Although there'd been a bit of disbelief in John's tone, he could picture Jonah doing such a thing. He was good with animals and they made Jonah happy.

"I followed him, of course."

A smile snapped to John's lips. "Of course." It was moments like these, when Brad went above and beyond the call of duty, that had John giving him huge Christmas bonuses.

Brad's evil grin notched up a hair. "He's volunteering at a place two blocks from his house, Perry Emergency Animal Services."

With his bottom lip held between his teeth, John turned inside himself. He'd known there was a real possibility Jonah would refuse Brad. He'd walked away without a word. One night wouldn't fix that. He had a backup plan, but he didn't know if he had time to pull it off. Not to mention, Jonah needed more in life than John. John had already proven all he had to offer was more of the same taking over of Jonah's life. With a sharp nod meant for himself, John snagged his phone and called the only person he trusted to help him. He had one thing he could offer Jonah that no one else could and she also happened to be a force of nature. Thankfully, she also happened to love Jonah as much as John did.

TWO OF THE longest hours of Jonah's life, working next to Tyrone, passed before he cracked. "John wants me back."

Tyrone froze. His gaze slid Jonah's way. He hadn't meant to blurt things out quite so intensely, but nervousness owned him. "And do you want him back?" Tyrone asked, sounding like he considered each word before speaking.

"I don't know." Jonah needed to be honest. He

didn't want any bad feelings between them. "I also don't want to hurt you, because I like you a lot."

A sexy smile stretched Tyrone's lips. "I know my chances are slim, so just talk it out with me. Pro con it. Let's hear it."

Jonah shook his head. "You're too nice for someone like me."

Tyrone snorted. "I've known from day one we're a case of bad timing. We met because of Cricket's passing, which is a lot like family dying. You told me right away you were just out of a three-year relationship and had just quit college. I know you have a lot going on. Otherwise, this other guy would have a real fight on his hands. I'm pretty persistent when I want someone."

Jonah's mouth went dry. He wasn't immune to the heat in Tyrone's stare. He cleared his throat. "I don't know where to start."

"Tell me about him," Tyrone prodded. "I promise no awkwardness. Sometimes, you don't know how you feel until you've said it out loud to someone."

That was true. Jonah nodded while keeping his gaze locked on the puppy he was feeding. "John is... the loudest voice at every party," Jonah said, pulling out the best description he could find. A smile tugged at Jonah's lips at the words. An image of John filled his head. "He's also the one who always picks up the check for every party. When we're together, he talks so much I never get to say anything, but I don't miss my voice when he's around. Every story he tells is hilarious. He's never met anyone who doesn't love him, even though he's overwhelming as hell." Once the flood gates opened, Jonah couldn't stop. "In the entirety of our relationship, I never ordered a meal for myself or picked a vacation spot. Yet I've never eaten anything I didn't want or gone somewhere I didn't love. John is so much larger than life, he just eclipses everything when he's around. I didn't even notice that I'd stopped existing until he was gone."

"Wow."

Jonah nodded at Tyrone's assessment. "Pretty much."

Tyrone leaned back against the counter and eyed Jonah. "That's a high pedestal you've built. It must've been a long fall for him."

Jonah kept his eyes averted. "I'm fairly certain I was just insulted, but that's nothing new for me."

"No," Tyrone said, straightening away from the counter. "I didn't mean it that way at all. What I mean is, when people get their heart broken, they go into survival mode. You're forced to look for the cracks in what you had together, because focusing on the good slowly kills you. If you wake up every day only remembering all the wonderful things you've lost, it's too hard. So you find the bad, even if it's the smallest thing that never occurred to you at the time. That's how you survive. The problem with that method of dealing with loss is what you're facing now. You picked John apart, hoping to get over him. Now, he wants you back, and you don't know how to unsee the cracks. That's all I meant," Tyrone explained. "Does that make sense?"

Jonah nodded. "That's a perfect assessment, actually." Without warning, Jonah's throat swelled. He swallowed past the lump. "I was happy, and I thought he was too. Then he was just gone. I don't want to spend the rest of my life waiting for it to happen again."

"Maybe it was a fluke."

"Maybe it was," Jonah said with a shrug. He blew out a sigh. "But he was all I had. Now I don't know what to do."

"Maybe you don't have to give John quite so much of yourself."

A smile exploded across Jonah's face. "Only someone who's never met John would ever say something like that. John is like a tornado. You have zero control from the moment he sweeps you away. I'll figure it out. I didn't mean to dump on you."

Tyrone's bright smile lit the room. "My life was pretty boring before you came along. You claim John is a tornado. I think you're a hurricane. You just kind of blew into my life and started rearranging things."

A chuckle rose in Jonah's throat. "That's probably the nicest thing anyone has ever said to me."

"You're also a weirdo," Tyrone said with a laugh.

Jonah shrugged. "There are worse things to be."

Tyrone's smile fell. "I hope if you decide to take John back you don't stop coming around. You know I'm a workaholic. I also don't have many friends. It's strange. I don't think I noticed anything lacking in my life until you pulled over for ice cream."

Jonah blinked against the sudden burning behind his eyes. "I was wrong. That was the nicest thing anyone has ever said to me. I won't stop coming around. As long as I'm welcome, I'd like to keep helping out."

"Maybe I should hire you."

"Not necessary," Jonah said as he rubbed the puppy's nose. "You're giving me more than you realize right now by letting me be here."

"I'm not surprised he wants you back." Tyrone's claim brought Jonah's gaze his way. "He'd be stupid not to, but make him squirm a little. Okay?"

Jonah winked and went back to watching the wiggling balls of fur inside the incubator. He had no intention of running back to John. Fallen from a pedestal or not, John had broken his heart. One night of hot sex hadn't changed that fact. Jonah wanted something real this time.

A quiet knock had Jonah and Tyrone turning toward the door. Jonah blinked in surprise at the sight of John's mother, Viv.

"There's my sweet baby. A very nice lady said I would find you back here."

"Viv." Seriously, it was all Jonah had. Viv's long silver hair hung over her shoulder. She was dressed to the nines in a pink suit Jonah knew cost well over a thousand dollars because he'd been with her when she'd bought it. She looked out of place in a vet's office surrounded by people in scrubs, Jonah included.

"Brad mentioned you were volunteering here." Jonah was almost positive he hadn't said exactly where he was volunteering. That meant Brad had followed him. Viv kept talking, preventing him from stating his irritation. "I heard about Cricket, baby," she said, sounding hurt on his behalf. "My heart breaks for you. I'm hoping you'll let me take you to lunch." Her light green gaze slid Tyrone's way. "If that's okay with you, of course. I don't want to steal away your help."

Jonah glanced Tyrone's way in time to catch his smile. "Jonah is a treasure. I can't stand in the way of him going to lunch with such a lovely lady."

"He's very good," Viv said, wagging her finger Tyrone's way while holding Jonah's stare. "Watch out for that one. The silver-tongued ones always wreck your life." She tossed Tyrone a wink. "Of course, that's not all they wreck, and it's always worth it."

Jonah blushed while Tyrone's sexy chuckle filled the air. He glanced down at himself. "I'm not dressed to match." Jonah knew from experience Viv had her son's taste and never dined anywhere cheap.

"Don't worry over that. You're so handsome it doesn't matter what you wear. Plus, anywhere I choose, they'll think you're a doctor on lunch."

If he was honest, Jonah didn't want to go. Not because he didn't like Viv. He loved her, but she belonged to John. If he didn't end up with John, he'd never see her again. That hurt. Jonah still couldn't tell her no. "Okay. Let me wash my hands

111

and we'll head out." Her open happiness made him smile. As he washed his hands, he could hear Tyrone and Viv talking in low tones behind him. The way Viv kept laughing had him fascinated and nervous. Tyrone didn't know Viv was John's mom. He didn't want Viv to find out about his date with Tyrone and think less of him. It didn't matter John had been the one to dump him. He cared what Viv thought of him.

"Are you ready?" Jonah asked, holding his elbow out to her like a gentleman. He loved the way things like that always seemed to make her happy. Jonah didn't have a mom. Not anymore. Sometimes, Viv felt like one. He'd tried not to think about her since John walked away. Jonah had lost so damn much lately.

"I'm always ready to hit the town with a handsome man." She paused before they cleared the door and glanced over her shoulder at Tyrone. "What about you, Dr. Perry? I'd love to make all the girls jealous with two handsome men escorting me."

"I don't want to intrude."

"Wash your hands, boy. I never do anything simply to avoid being rude. Always accept a free lunch from an old lady. We're not promised a tomorrow. Plus, my sons, John and Jude, have ensured I'll never have grandchildren, so I have to get my kicks elsewhere."

Jonah fought a wince when he saw Tyrone hesitate as Viv's words sank in. Tyrone's gaze moved Jonah's way. "Um."

"For God's sake, boy. I'm not getting any younger. Let's go."

"Yes, ma'am," Tyrone said, giving in gracefully. He quickly washed his hands and opened the door for them as they headed for the parking lot.

Jonah met his gaze as he passed. "Sorry," Jonah mouthed, horrified.

Tyrone winked, stealing some of the misery from Jonah. "Would you like me to drive?" Tyrone offered.

Viv shook her head. "I invited you. That means I pay, and I drive. Plus, I have one quick stop to make before we eat. I hope that's okay."

"Of course," Tyrone said, being more than congenial, considering he was always on call.

With Viv holding on to his arm, Jonah led the way to her BMW Gran Coupe. When they moved close, the doors automatically unlocked, and Jonah opened the driver's side door for her. Once she was behind the wheel, he closed her inside and circled the car. Tyrone stood waiting with the passenger side door held open for Jonah. Jonah's heart smiled. Even though Tyrone knew they were leaving with John's mother, he still hadn't completely conceded to John yet.

"Thank you," Jonah said, fighting a blush as he slid inside.

Viv didn't waste the split second they had alone between Tyrone closing the door and getting in the back seat. "Oh, he's hot. My son had better get his shit together."

Jonah's blush intensified, but he kept his mouth shut. The longer they drove, the more familiar the neighborhood became. A terrible feeling grew inside Jonah, but he didn't fully accept the horrible truth until Viv pulled into the driveway of the home where he'd grown up.

"No." It was all Jonah could push past his tight throat.

"I'll only be a second."

Viv's reassurance helped nothing. "No," he repeated, managing to sound a hair more forceful this time.

"What?" Tyrone asked, sounding lost.

Viv threw open her door.

"This is my mother's house," Jonah explained as he scrambled out of the car to run after Viv.

The evil-looking joy on Viv's face scared the hell out of Jonah as she stormed toward the door. Short of tackling her, there was no way for Jonah to stop Viv before she rang the doorbell. He watched in horror as she pressed the button that sent chimes clanging through the house. Life had never taken mercy on him before and let him melt into the ground. It didn't happen today either.

His mom opened the door. "Yes?" She spoke before her gaze slid Jonah's way. When she spotted him, her lips snapped together. Jonah's throat swelled near to closing at the sound of the single word. It was the first word he'd heard in his mother's voice in five long years. Even though it hadn't been meant for him, it sliced through his heart.

"We don't know each other," Viv said, pulling his mom's gaze back her way. "But we have someone in common. My son tells me you no longer want yours. I'm here to inform you I'm taking the job." Jonah's gaze snapped to Viv and didn't move. Tears sprang to his eyes. Viv didn't stop or back down. "Obviously, I'm quite a bit older than you. In truth, I'm closer to being old enough to be Jonah's grandmother, but seeing as how you tossed him aside, he'll have to settle for me. But I can't live with myself if I don't tell you, one mother to another, you're a piece of shit and you don't deserve such an amazing son." His mom tried closing the door in Viv's face. Proving she was stronger than she looked, Viv threw out her hand, stopping her. "No doubt, if you ever decide to come crawling back, Jonah will forgive you, because he's everything amazing that you are not. Until then, he belongs to my family now, and I hope you burn in Hell. Go with God," Viv said with a sharp nod. With a flounce, Viv snagged his arm and headed back toward the car. She didn't look his way, but Jonah couldn't take his eyes off her. He never looked back. Viv held his attention. His throat hurt too badly to say anything.

At the driver's side door, Viv finally met his stare. He realized then her eyes were filled with tears. He imagined he looked the same. She touched Jonah's cheek. "Don't you ever let anyone toss you aside again. Whether my son pulls his shit together or not, you're one of mine. You always have a place with me. Now move that ass and get in the car. I have lots of old biddies to make jealous at the club."

Oh, lord. They were having lunch at Viv's club. Nothing was ever free. He'd have to endure an hour getting his ass pinched by old ladies. Viv was worth it, though. There wasn't much he wouldn't do for her now that she was his new mom.

EIGHT

LUNCH WAS BLESSEDLY SHORT THANKS TO Tyrone having appointments for the rest of the afternoon. After making plans to go shopping with Viv for the upcoming weekend and promising Tyrone he'd come back tomorrow to help with the puppies, Jonah headed across the parking lot. Before Jonah made it to his car, he spotted the note and a single rose waiting for him beneath his windshield wiper. Fucking John. Jonah was already smiling. He automatically brought the flower to his nose as he read.

Your favorite color is red. That's why I bought the red Hummer and almost exclusively buy you red roses.

With a shake of his head, Jonah slipped behind the wheel. There was a post-it note on his radio, surprising a chuckle from him.

You hate my music. I think yours sucks too.

Jonah laughed again. He started the car and drove home on autopilot. John was relentless. Jonah already knew the man wouldn't stop at two notes. As he pulled into the driveway, he could already see the bright yellow paper stuck to his front door. Jonah forced himself to walk at a normal pace, but there was no stopping his smile as pulled open the screen door.

You didn't want this door.

Jonah's throat swelled. He couldn't believe John remembered that. When John bought the house, it had a beautiful glass door Jonah loved. John replaced it with wood because he wanted Jonah safe. As Jonah pushed the door open, he spotted sticky notes everywhere. He moved to the closest one. It was on the floor. Jonah picked it up.

I was standing right here the moment I realized I'm in love with you. You were folding socks and explaining how you can tell the difference between right and left socks.

The tightness in Jonah's throat increased. He trailed through the house, inspecting each note.

When I got here, you'd been crying and wouldn't tell me why. So I made love to you right here. You never looked away from me the entire time.

You have an odd fascination for vampires.

Your favorite scent is apricot.

I bought shoes you hated so much you hid them from me. FYI, I've always known they're in the pool house, but I'd never wear something you hate.

By the time Jonah made it to his bedroom, he held a ton of tiny sticky notes. His mouth fell open when he spotted his bed. The entire headboard was covered in notes. He crawled onto the bed and skimmed a few.

This is where I wait until you're asleep to tell you I love you.

You snore. It's adorable.

You talk in your sleep. Sometimes, that's not adorable.

I miss you so much it's choking me. When I realized I was the reason you wouldn't graduate, I thought I was ruining your life. So I ruined mine to save you, but I'm drowning without you.

A tear rolled down Jonah's cheek. He swiped it away and leapt from the bed. His steps didn't slow. Later, he'd take the time to read every single note. For now, he'd seen as much as he needed to see. His heart beat so fast on the drive to John's house, he thought he might faint. There were thousands of places John could be. Jonah felt John in his soul. He was at home. Jonah didn't bother heading for the garage. He parked in the front. The bright white envelope taped to the door called his name. Jonah's chest heaved like he'd run all the way there as he plucked the card from the door. Inside, he found a card with red roses on the front. He flipped it open.

This is the home I should've offered you.

Jonah pushed the door open. He already knew it would be unlocked. Desperation to get to John ate at Jonah's mind. He smiled as the trail of rose petals came into view. They were red, of course. Jonah kept his gaze locked on the marble floor, following the line to a set of glass French doors that led outside. He left the card and his phone on the table by the door. Once he stepped outside, he nearly groaned. A light flickered behind the waterfall pouring into the pool. There was an alcove behind the waterfall where John kept another three-person lounge. The problem was there was only one way to get there. Swim. The tiny light flickered again. With the sun setting behind the large alcove of rocks, the flickering light became more apparent. It looked like candles. Short of a drone flying over, there was no chance of anyone seeing into John's backyard. It was built to look like a jungle with a swimming pool and waterfall in the center.

Jonah walked to the edge of the pool. He couldn't see John behind the rushing water, but Jonah could feel him. John was there, just out of sight and watching. While relishing the idea of John waiting, anticipating, Jonah reached for the hem of his shirt and slowly lifted it over his head, dragging out the show. He dropped the material at his feet before toeing off his shoes and removing his socks. Jonah pulled the string on the bottom half of his scrubs, untying them. He pushed them down his hips, taking his underwear with them. Jonah could've dove in. Instead, he walked to the stairs and descended into the pool one step at a time. Warm water lapped at his skin. He didn't rush. Jonah swore he could feel John's heated stare caressing his skin. When he dipped through the cascading water and slicked his wet hair back, Jonah wasn't disappointed. John sat, hungry-eyed and waiting. Candles surrounded the lounge.

"I was beginning to think you wouldn't show."

Jonah folded his arms on the edge of the pool and

set his chin on his forearm. "Have I ever given you a reason to doubt me?"

"Not even once." The sincerity in John's voice warmed Jonah's heart. "Do you plan to stay in the water?"

Jonah shrugged. "You forced me to give up my clothes to see you. I might get cold."

John stood and grabbed a thick towel. Jonah ate up the sight of John's huge body in nothing but swimming trunks. He was so fucking gorgeous. The man always stole Jonah's breath. His massive chest and arms always made Jonah feel safe while engulfing him. Jonah didn't want to lose that. John moved to the edge of the pool and held the towel open for Jonah. "I have the perfect spot to keep you warm."

Heat grew inside Jonah as he pushed from the pool and walked into John's waiting arms. He wrapped Jonah in the towel before urging him onto the lounge. John held his stare as he climbed in beside him and gathered Jonah into his embrace. It was like coming home. Jonah would've agreed to anything in that moment, as long as he could keep John.

"I have something I need to say."

Trepidation struck Jonah at John's serious tone. "Okay."

"I love you."

Jonah pressed his lips together, trying to hold back a squeal. Only when he had his heart under control did he respond. "I love you too."

John released his breath. It sounded ragged, making Jonah realize exactly how nervous John truly was. Jonah's heart turned over in his chest. Before that moment, it hadn't occurred to him that John didn't know he was Jonah's whole world. That—one day—John had consumed him, and Jonah hadn't looked back.

Jonah held John's stare and prayed he could make John believe what everyone else already knew with one look at Jonah when he was with John. "It's not the money. I don't want another contract. I don't want to be a deal you make. A bargain you can walk away from. I don't give a damn if you never spend another dime on me. Just don't abandon me again."

A line appeared between John's brows. Pain etched his features. "How could you want me at all? I took over your life. If you ever had any dreams for yourself, I never bothered to learn what they are." John shook his head. His gaze dropped to where he toyed with Jonah's fingers. "It's like I'm too in love with being with you. I can't stop telling you every thought in my head and overwhelming everything else in your life—like I can't control it."

"Have you ever heard me complain?"

A humorless laugh escaped John. "Have I given you a chance to?"

Jonah bumped John's chin with his fingertips, forcing him to lift his gaze. A smile pulled at Jonah's lips as John's sexy green stare hit his. He couldn't stop himself from stealing a quick peck on the lips. He dove in, pressing his lips to John's before backing away just as fast. John's serious expression didn't break. Jonah gave him a sharp nod. He needed John to take him seriously for another minute. "If you ever disappear on me again, I won't be the adult next time. I'll key your car."

A sexy-sounding chuckle escaped John, but Jonah wasn't finished.

"I'm one hundred percent serious, John. I'll poison your lawn and take an ad out in the paper, telling the world how much I hurt. You haven't seen low until you've seen me sink. I'll spray paint your house. You'll have to call the cops."

John laughed harder. "Stop."

Jonah shook his head. "I'm not done. We've done things your way, and it was cruel." John's laughter died. Jonah kept going. "Silence is the most painful and insulting blow someone who loves you can deliver. That's one thing I need you to understand and never do to me again. I've spent five years begging my own mother to speak to me or even look at me. It's an issue for me and I felt like you did the same thing. You just cut me from your life." Jonah shook his head again. "It was the cruelest thing you could've chosen to do. So, yeah. I'll stalk you. You'll wish you never came back. If you don't really want to be back, you should say so now. I'm not afraid of you overwhelming me. I'm terrified you'll disappear."

"I want another contract. One that protects you."

A growl rose in Jonah's throat at John's claim. It was like John wasn't hearing him. "I love you, John. You. Not the money or the house or the trips. You." A rant built inside Jonah. He was ready to drown John with it.

A ring appeared beneath his nose. Jonah couldn't look away from the platinum and diamonds. "I want another contract, Jonah. One that'll tie you to me for life this time."

As Jonah stared at the ring, peace settled over him. The first pure breath of oxygen he'd taken in years filled his lungs. In that moment, he recognized he was home.

EVERY NERVE in John's body drew up taut as he watched Jonah stare at the ring. Everything rode on Jonah's answer. Before Jonah, John had never experienced the slightest desire to ever marry. Now he couldn't picture his life without this man who completely owned him. In fact, spending time without Jonah, thinking he'd never get to touch him, hear his voice, or smell his skin again had been like his worst nightmare come true.

John couldn't take it. "What do you say? Will you marry me?"

Jonah finally blinked. His gaze slid John's way. "No."

The blow landed harder than John could have ever expected. He swore he heard his heart shatter, and it was almost impossible to breathe. Still, he didn't blame Jonah. "That makes sense. I mean, I'm a lot older than you and you shouldn't tie yourself to me after everything I've done."

"Jesus," Jonah muttered. "You're a complete idiot. You know that, right? How could you think I don't want you?" He waved for the ring. "Gimme, gimme."

Even as John slid the ring on Jonah's finger, he

still hadn't recovered from the shock of Jonah's no. Before that moment, he hadn't realized how much he'd come to depend on Jonah always saying yes. "It looks perfect on you." Even John heard the sadness tinging his voice.

Jonah's gaze met his. "You can have the ring back and I'll happily marry you without it if that'll take the unhappiness from your eyes."

John shook his head. "It's not that. You deserve a different ring for every day, but am I what's best for you? When I first found that website, it was all about being stupid and throwing my money around."

"Playing the field with as many people as you could buy," Jonah finished for him, making things sound so much worse.

"Don't rub it in, boy. I'm pouring my heart out here."

Jonah pressed his lips together, showing his obedience in the most obnoxious way he could. John didn't care as long Jonah let him speak his piece. "I'm trying to say I never expected you. Everything about us was all in fun at first. We did a lot of shit together I would never do now, but do you know I would never do those things? Do you realize I'm not me without you?"

Jonah's steady gaze never wavered. He didn't

backdown from John pouring out his heart. "I don't know who you are without me, but I know before you pulled your disappearing act, you'd never let me down. You're right. We've done a lot of shit together I would never do again. At first, for a while, I went along with things I didn't want, and when my life started falling apart, you ghosted on me. I won't lie and say I'm over that last one. But if you need to know what's best for me, I absolutely believe it's you. You have no idea how deep I had to dig to find any issues with our relationship when you left." Jonah shrugged. "I just love you too much to feel anything else. How can that be wrong for me?"

"I'd give anything to take back my stupidity." John had never meant anything more. "You're getting the grandest wedding the world has ever seen. Seriously, I'm putting rich kids' sweet sixteen parties to shame. You'll have magazines wanting to cover this shit."

Jonah shifted and straddled John's hips. His towel slipped away in the move, leaving John's swim trunks as nowhere near enough protection. Jonah cupped his face. "No."

John blinked. He didn't understand. "What do you mean no? You've been throwing that word around a little too much."

A sexy-sounding chuckle escaped Jonah, but he didn't let up. "We're having an elegant, intimate wedding with family and friends. No magazines or crazy over-the-top bs. I don't want a circus. What I want is to marry the greatest love of my life without our vows being upstaged by the spectacle our wedding has become. Okay?"

John fought back a laugh. "Anything you want, it's yours."

A heated glance slid down John's body, stirring his cock. "What I want is already beneath me. The question is, what should I do with you?"

An unsteady breath escaped John. Jonah had a way of taking him from nothing to ready to fly in an instant. The overwhelming emotions never got old. "Whatever you want."

Jonah's fingertips dipped inside John's shorts and skimmed his crown. His stare never wavered from John's. "I want to watch you come."

John thought Jonah would probably see it sooner rather than later, talking like that. His head fell back against the chair as Jonah freed his erection. Air became scarce as Jonah's fingers encircled him. Jonah pumped. John fought to breathe. With one hand braced on the back of the chair over John's head, Jonah dropped his chin and watched as he jacked off John. John couldn't look away from Jonah. They were getting married posthaste. He already knew he wouldn't tolerate a long engagement. The idea of having Jonah as his husband was already in his head. John didn't have the patience to wait. Possessiveness mixed with lust. John tried breathing past the explosive combo. Then Jonah went to work, stripping away John's shorts and leaving nothing between them. They were skin on skin. Jonah's bare ass was on John's lap. The warmth seeped into his skin, making John insane with desire. His fingers dug into Jonah's ass cheeks. He fought the urge to take control.

Jonah slid closer until their erections met. With his palm still braced on the back of the chair, Jonah got his feet beneath him until he was squatting on John's lap. Completely in control now, Jonah moved against John. John held Jonah's ass and helped set the pace as Jonah stroked their dicks and rubbed them together, causing a friction that made John insane. Jonah threw his head back and visibly sucked air while driving them both crazy. He massaged and humped, fucking John with no penetration. John was transfixed. Every ounce of his being remained focused on the sensation of their cocks moving against each other. It was enough, but then again, it wasn't. He fought the urge to bury his dick in Jonah's tight, hot ass. As much as he wanted that, he didn't want to stop this.

Jonah's hips rotated. His speed increased, and his low moans got louder. John couldn't even blink. He didn't want to miss a second of Jonah taking his pleasure. The spring inside John wound slowly tighter. His fingertips kept massaging Jonah's ass and moving closer to what he wanted without thought until he was fingering Jonah's asshole without mercy. He needed Jonah's orgasm. John knew it would be beautiful. Jonah's gaze hit his. His cheeks were flushed, making his sweet light-brown eyes seem even brighter than usual.

Jonah's bottom lip was held between his teeth. John had never seen a sexier sight. Then, a loud gasp escaped Jonah and hot cum coated John's body. The sight ripped an orgasm from John with enough force it tore a cry from his throat. Jonah claimed his mouth. Their tongues clashed as their racing hearts fought to get closer to each other. John's chest swelled with pride even as tears pressed at the backs of his eyes. The magnitude of the day landed on his shoulders. This man would soon be John's husband. Their lives would change in all the best ways. If Jonah thought John was over-the-top while they were dating, he hadn't seen a damn thing yet. John planned to rain down so much happiness on Jonah, he'd forget what it was like to frown. For the rest of their lives, John would protect Jonah from every ugliness in life. This was forever.

NINE

THE RED BRICK BUILDING WHERE JONAH volunteered almost daily was a tiny place. John assumed, since there was only one vet inside, they didn't take on a lot of animals at once. Being as how they were the only emergency clinic for miles, John also assumed Tyrone rarely got any sleep but made decent money. As John cleared the door, the blonde woman who worked the front desk smiled and waved him toward the back without question. Everyone who worked there was nice and used to seeing John hanging around. The main area off the waiting room was a large room with an examination table, sink and counter. There were several smaller rooms for appointments, while the main room served as a stopping point to assess the seriousness of each animal's condition before moving to the back. John spotted Jonah the moment he passed through the doorway leading to the back. He was down on one knee, running his hands down the back of a dog with a cast on its leg.

"You're such a sweet guy," Jonah said in a baby voice. John couldn't look away. Jonah looked damn sexy in scrubs and this place brought out the happiness in his eyes. "Daddy says I can't bring home another baby."

"Are you seriously throwing me under the bus right now?"

Jonah jumped and spun at the sound of John's voice. The way his eyes lit as they landed on John stole John's breath. There was nothing he wouldn't do to ensure Jonah kept looking at him the way he was now. "Well, I have to tell him something," Jonah said, continuing to pet the huge husky he'd been babying as John cleared the doorway of the vet clinic. Jonah covered the dog's ears. "I can't tell him I don't want another dog. That's just mean. He'll think something is wrong with him."

John chuckled at the idea of Jonah sparing a dog's feelings. "This isn't the pound. I'm assuming he already has an owner."

"He does," Tyrone said, appearing behind Jonah

with a clipboard in hand. "That doesn't stop all the animals from wanting to go home with Jonah."

"I understand the sentiment," John said with a serious tone. There was nowhere he'd rather be.

Abandoning the dog, Jonah crossed the room. The moment he reached John's side, he went up on his toes and claimed John's lips. John hauled him closer, uncaring of anyone watching. Jonah chuckled against his mouth. "What brings you by, sexy?"

"I couldn't stay away," John admitted. Since Jonah had taken him back and accepted his marriage proposal three months earlier, John had tried to do better about letting Jonah have a life outside of him. It was easier with Jonah living with him. No matter how life pulled them in different directions during the day, Jonah was in his arms at night. Still, there were times when the desire to see Jonah outweighed everything and John still crashed his way in. "I'd hoped I could talk you into going to lunch with me. Maybe Tyrone could join us too if he's free." Even though Jonah had confessed to going on a date with the man he now volunteered for, John tried to befriend the guy. It wasn't like John could blame Tyrone for trying, and he trusted Jonah. Not to mention hell would freeze before John ever gave Jonah a reason to go elsewhere.

Jonah snaked his arm around John's waist and turned Tyrone's way. "What do you say, Ty? An extremely handsome man has offered to treat us to lunch. Do you think we can spare a minute for him?"

Tyrone checked his wrist. "Shit. I keep forgetting my watch broke." He pulled his phone from his pocket and checked the time. "It looks like I have time. My next appointment isn't for another two-and-a-half hours. Barring any unforeseen emergencies, we should be good."

John sneaked in another kiss behind Jonah's ear before he scampered away to wash up. With one shoulder leaned against the doorframe, John watched Jonah's ass while he waited. He really loved the scrubs. Even John's heart smiled as he listened to Jonah chatter happily about his day. Occasionally, Tyrone chimed in with an extra detail, but Jonah was the one who held the floor as John drove to a restaurant they loved.

He spotted a familiar market and pulled to the shoulder of the road. "Oops. Hold that thought, baby. I almost forgot something." John rushed across the road to the store. He knew from experience this particular place always carried the freshest red roses. Jonah needed flowers in his life. John didn't want to make

Tyrone and Jonah wait for long, but they needed gifts. After grabbing a dozen roses for Jonah, John searched the aisles for something that fit Tyrone. He almost gave up when he spotted a glass case at the register and smiled. Gifts in hand, John ran back for the SUV.

As he slid behind the wheel, he passed the flowers Jonah's way. "For the love of my life." It never got old watching Jonah light up with happiness. He almost hated to look away as Jonah brought the roses to his nose.

"Thank you, baby."

John handed the bag he held back to Tyrone. "And for you."

Tyrone waved off the gift, looking embarrassed. "Oh, no. You don't need to give me anything."

Before John's hackles rose, Jonah stepped in. "Take the gift, sweetie. It's important to John."

Tyrone's shoulders fell. He reached for the bag and peered inside. With a shake of his head, he pulled the watch from the bag. A soft laugh escaped him. "You bought me a watch."

"Yep," John said, pulling away from the curb. "You said yours broke. Problem solved."

Jonah stroked his hand. John glanced his way in time for Jonah to toss him a wink. Even though the gift had been for Tyrone, it was always Jonah's reaction he sought.

"This was very nice of you. Thank you." The words coming from the backseat were so quietly spoken John almost didn't hear them. He cast a quick look at the rear-view mirror and caught a glimpse of Tyrone's expression. He looked sad. John shook it off. He'd have the man smiling again before long. John didn't believe in letting people be unhappy.

Thankfully, the restaurant seated them quickly. They'd barely skimmed the menu when a shadow fell over the table. John glanced up to find a smiling David.

"Finally. I think this is the first time I've seen the two of you in one place in ages."

Jonah bounced a little. "Mr. Baker."

"Just David."

Jonah ignored the admonishment as always. "How have you been? You should join us."

David cast a look around the table as if worried he'd be intruding. John rushed to reassure him. "Seriously, David. Join us. We've been crazy busy with the wedding planning, but we've missed you."

"In that case," David said with a nod. He slid into the booth next to Tyrone. "David Baker," he added, holding his hand out for Tyrone.

Tyrone accepted his handshake. "Tyrone Perry."

David eyed Tyrone's scrubs and lab coat. "Doctor?"

"Veterinarian."

"That's a great calling."

Tyrone looked slightly taken aback by the compliment. "Thank you." No doubt it looked to have come from just another snobbish California rich dude. While David did have more money than God, he also was more of a glorified farmer than anything else. He lived on hundreds of acres of farmland and owned a stable of horses. John was certain there were other animals running around as well.

David nodded before focusing on John and Jonah. "I got your wedding invitation. It made my day. I can't think of two people more meant for each other."

"Awww, thank you," Jonah cooed. "You have to save a dance for me at the reception. Who are you bringing?"

"Hmmm," David said, looking suddenly uncomfortable. "I have no idea. My life is pretty much work and nothing else."

"That's a feeling I know well," Tyrone said, chiming in.

David looked his way again. "Do you have a date for the big day?"

John's gaze moved between the two. The memory of Tyrone's expression after seeing John's gift filled John's head. He spoke before bothering to consider his words. "You two should come together."

Tyrone dropped his gaze to the table as if embarrassed. David looked away. "I'm sure Tyrone would prefer to go with someone closer to his age."

"Oh, I don't know," Tyrone said, bringing David's gaze back his way. "I think we could have fun. What time should I pick you up?"

The way David blinked in surprise had John fighting back laughter. "You want to pick me up?"

Tyrone gave a sharp nod as if the decision solidified in his mind. "Yeah. I'd love to take you if you're willing."

"All right. Let me give you my number."

John glanced Jonah's way as the pair across from them exchanged numbers. Jonah was already staring at him. John's hand lifted without thought. His thumb traced Jonah's bottom lip. The rest of the world fell away. A happy sigh rose in John's chest. Sometimes, John wondered if there would come a day when his emotions weren't as powerful when he looked at Jonah. He doubted it. After all, three years had passed, and his feelings only got stronger every day.

"I love you," he silently mouthed, needing to release some of the building pressure.

Jonah smiled as he returned the words. "I love you too." John's knuckles ran down Jonah's cheek, tracing the line. The whole room could've been staring, and John never would've noticed. His entire being focused on one grand plan. They would be happy like this for the rest of their lives, and they were.

Keep an eye out for the next Sugar Daddy, *Sugar Obsession.*

Please consider leaving a review at the retailer where this book was purchased. Reviews really help with a book's visibility, which ensures I can continue writing. Thank you, Charity.

ABOUT THE AUTHOR

Charity Parkerson is an award winning and multi-published author with several companies. Born with no filter from her brain to her mouth, she decided to take this odd quirk and insert it in her characters.

*Eight-time Readers' Favorite Award Winner
    *2015 Passionate Plume Award Finalist
    *2013 Reviewers' Choice Award Winner
    *2012 ARRA Finalist for Favorite Paranormal Romance
    *Five-time winner of The Mistress of the Darkpath

Connect with her online:

--Join my street team: facebook.com/TeamCharityParkerson
    --Sign up for my newsletter: http://bit.ly/CharityNews

--Website: charityparkerson.com

--Facebook:

facebook.com/authorCharityParkerson

facebook.com/TheMenofSin

--Twitter: twitter.com/CharityParkerso